the saving of
VERANO

KEN HELFER

RED CLIFFS
PUBLISHING

The Saving of Verano: The Verano Series
Published by Red Cliffs Publishing
Durango, CO

Publisher's Cataloging-in-Publication data
Names: Helfer, Ken, author.
Title: The saving of Verano / Ken Helfer.
Description: Durango, CO: Red Cliffs Publishing, 2022| Series: Verano series ; book 1.
Identifiers: ISBN 979-8-9858887-0-6
Subjects: LCSH Human-alien encounters--Fiction. | Outer space--Exploration--Fiction. | Science fiction. | BISAC FICTION / Science Fiction / Alien Contact
Classification: LCC PS3608.E388 S38 2022 | DDC 813.6--dc23

Cover and interior design by Creative Reflections, Developmental Editing by Kristen Corrects, and Copy line & Proof editing by Jennifer Bisbing, copyright owned by Ken Helfer.

For Emily, Aurora, Shane, and Trenton
In loving memory of Randy Tribble

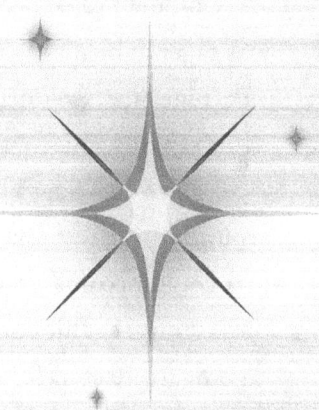

PROLOGUE

EARLY TWENTY-FIRST CENTURY

SOON AFTER his inauguration, and before the many parties he would attend as guest of honor, President Hartman met with his national security advisor for the initial presidential briefing. He was finally in a position to know the government secrets that, to most, were just conspiracy theories. The daily presidential briefing was in a format the new president felt most comfortable with. Barack Obama liked to read his as an in-depth report in a leather-bound notebook at the breakfast table. JFK read his first briefing sitting on the diving board at his Hyannis Port residence. LBJ had his read to him as he sat on the porcelain throne.

President Hartman preferred to be briefed in person, at breakfast, and then reread the most salient points while on an exercise bike at some point during the day.

"Good morning, Mr. President. How are you today?"

The president picked up his fork.

Colonel Frank Bronson, ever the consummate professional soldier, was eager to begin.

"Fine, fine, Colonel. What have you got for me?" asked the president, while sampling his first White House breakfast.

"We're watching a new viral outbreak in Chad. Our people are on the ground trying to monitor events and determine if it's an airborne virus that could become a pandemic. As you know, we're still recovering from the last one that hit us out of China with no warning. Some of the fallout is going to affect us for a long time."

As the colonel kept talking, the president knew America, and the world faced serious and existential threats. The industrial-military complex, along with corporate media, had set most major policy goals for over a generation. Warlord capitalism took Earth's resources—air, water, forests, the oceans—for themselves while the people were fighting the orchestrated "Culture Wars."

But the worst and most threatening problem President Hartman would attempt to face was the looming specter of global climate change and loss of biodiversity.

The greenhouse gases, CO_2 and methane, were now at concentrations of well over 425 ppb in the atmosphere, something not seen in hundreds of thousands of years on Earth, and definitely not in the 10,000 years of human civilization. Coastal flooding, forest fires, melting permafrost, all spelled serious and rapid decline of many ecosystems and species. And, like the canary in the coal mine, as they went, so, too, would humans.

We're in real trouble, the president thought. *But damn it, we won't go down doing jack about it!*

Colonel Bronson was wrapping up when the president said, "One more thing, Colonel. I have a personal interest in finding out the truth about UFOs. I saw one long ago as a young man and would like some confirmation as to what it might have been."

The colonel was silent, listening.

"I was hunting with friends in the backwoods when we heard a whoosh above us. We looked up and saw a huge, slow-moving craft gliding silently overhead. The speed was far too slow for an object its size; we knew it couldn't stay airborne and was going to crash. The three of us jumped into the truck and headed down the old logging road we were on toward what would be the imminent crash site. I was sitting shotgun, yelling instructions to my friend Roscoe—when suddenly the craft went straight up, turned 180 degrees, and flew back over the truck—so fast it was just a dark blur and then disappeared. We all swore like sailors and looked at each other in utter disbelief at what we had just seen. Now, at long last, I want to know what is going on. Are we being visited by aliens?"

Colonel Bronson reached into his briefcase and handed the president a laptop. "I don't know much about the Foo Fighters myself, but this level of file is given to incoming presidents for a reason, and if you had not asked about it, I would have left it with you anyway. Only the current president and the joint chiefs have a high enough clearance to watch this. We have reason to believe every leader in the world with access to nukes received the same greeting. Once the file is opened, it will self-erase after twenty-four hours. Thank you, Mr. President. See you next week." He saluted and left the White House.

Foo Fighters. Hartman knew bomber crews used to see them over Europe in WWII. That was a long time ago now, and it was high time the mystery got exposed once and for all.

He perused the report. Words like *aliens*, *arrival*, and *danger* jumped out on the page at him.

If people knew there were intelligent beings somewhere out there, it might cause them to pull together as one Earth. On the other hand, knowing human nature, some would try to curry favor with them and turn on their own. Hopefully, the aliens had benign intentions.

A FEW DAYS LATER, after the whirlwind of inauguration activity settled down, President Hartman decided to open the file. He made sure there would be no interruptions by staff or family, sat down at the Resolute Desk in the Oval Office, and pushed play.

A squadron of four F-35s, flying in formation, came on the screen. Hartman leaned forward, paying attention. It was not the usual out-of-focus or grainy UFO footage, but a clear image of a flying disk moving at the same speed as the fighters but just above them. In a flash it was behind them, pointing a beam of light on all four planes at once.

President Hartman watched the footage, waiting for whatever happened next.

The disk shot past them, clearly at speeds Hartman could only imagine. In the distance, the disk stopped dead, hovering. The lead fighter, believing they had been targeted by the alien craft, fired an AMRAAM air-to-air, laser-guided missile, which headed straight for the UFO. A nanosecond before impact, the disk flew straight up and disappeared into the stratosphere.

Air Force General Kurt Weller addressed the camera, "Mr. President, obviously the aliens are toying with us *and* have capabilities far beyond our own. We have plenty of dramatic footage like this one, but they don't seem hostile. What you are about to hear is a recording sent by the aliens right after SpaceX announced their intention of going to Mars."

The screen went blank and a calm voice, with an American accent, started to speak:

I address the leaders of planet Earth in your own languages. I serve as Planetary Ranger in this remote region of the galaxy. Earth became a planet of concern, when long-range quantum sensors picked up nuclear explosions in Earth year 1945. I visited in order to determine what level of exposure the galaxy at large might have to your emerging civilization. I have been studying your planet and humans anew and have found much to appreciate. Yours is such a magnificent planet, and humans are a courageous and creative people. I'm fascinated by your art, music, and the light shining from your eyes. You have adequate intelligence and may someday find your place among the space-faring civilizations in this vast, far-flung galaxy.

But there is also poverty, disease, war, and immense suffering inflicted on the weak and many of your planet's sentient animals. You have allowed the greedy and powerful to rule for profit, and you might lose your biosphere, possibly going extinct altogether.

For those reasons, I am not the only one interested in the Earth. There are others, and they do not believe humans are able to evolve. It is their crafts you see regularly, and trust me when I say, you are no match for them. I will protect you for now, but I implore you to act on your many pressing problems before it is too late.

I understand that your scientists believe faster-than-light travel to be against the laws of physics. But I must tell you, indeed, there is a way to move throughout the galaxy, and you will eventually discover it. At such time, you will be prevented from leaving your solar system until I can be sure you are not bringing destruction with you. I cannot and will not help you or save you. Humanity must save itself. Yes, you possess intelligence, but far more importantly, your hearts are genuinely unique, and you must find them. I do believe you have a chance to find your way, and know that my deepest hopes are with you.

CHAPTER
ONE

TWENTY SEVENTH CENTURY

SELBY RICKS' SADNESS from the loss returned, as he remembered the day everything changed. He had been studying to be a biodiversity engineer so that he could follow in the footsteps of his famous parents. Like them, he wanted to dedicate his life to the science of better understanding the Earth and the complex web of life it sustains.

Almost a year ago now, the accident happened. He and his parents were snowboarding in the backcountry near Ophir Pass. It was a day with bluebird skies and three feet of fresh, light powder, making for perfect snow conditions. They were having a blast, just so grateful snowfall was returning to the mountains most years now.

All three were trained search and rescue volunteers who knew the dangers of avalanches, but as they cut across an old chute, Selby heard a deafening roar and looked up to see a white wall coming at them. He gasped. *There's no way we can survive it*, he thought, his eyes widening at the wall of white before him. *It's too close.*

His dad shouted, "Run for it!"

Selby felt, but could not see, his board head downhill. Even though he knew outrunning an avalanche is next to impossible.

Blinded, he only felt the wave of white barrel down on him. When he was caught, it tumbled him head over heels down the slope. He grunted as he was tossed around like a ragdoll. What was only a few seconds seemed like an eternity.

As suddenly as it started, the roar was replaced by complete silence. He lay there, in a white world, trying to decide which way was up. His training caused him to instinctively form an air pocket and to send a thought to his phone to alert Search and Rescue. It looked slightly light to his right, so he started swimming through the snow toward it, emerging after a few minutes, coughing and sputtering.

Knowing he had been lucky and now desperate to find his parents, he searched for signs of them as he heard the rescue drones approach. His parents had also alerted Search, and their phone beacon showed their locations.

The drones hovered over the area his parents were in and started a rescue, which turned into a recovery of the bodies. They had been buried too deep and had suffocated.

Selby forced himself back to the present moment and took a deep breath. He felt little movement, but out a window, he could see the ground slowly recede. The last few weeks had been a whirlwind as he packed and said his goodbyes before going to school on Mars. He had planned to be a biosphere reclamation specialist. Growing up in his hometown of Telluride, Colorado, he had been told the stories of horrible fires in the western half of North America during the climate meltdown of the twenty-first and twenty-second centuries. Every tree in California had burned from the warming climate, including the giant Sequoias, and in the mountain areas like Colorado, most alpine forests burned up to the

10,000 feet elevation. Though much of the earth had been re-wilded, there was still work to be done.

But pursuing his original life plan seemed somewhat empty now, and he felt the need to find a different path. So, when his Uncle Carson told him about a medic training program in space survival, he signed up.

He was nineteen years old. Young enough to allow his thirst for adventure to overcome the disorientation of leaving the only home he had ever known. Like many other kids, his childhood had been spent learning to be self-sufficient and productive in a field or fields of interest. Long gone were the days of sitting in school year after year training to be both worker and consumer in a global economy. Not being groomed to work for a living, left time for children to learn the things AI could not do for them. Foremost was critical thinking as well as learning about the true self.

Creating art, playing music, learning to act, playing sports, or just having fun were the pursuits children were encouraged to pursue. Selby had learned guitar and studied music history. He played Robert Johnson, Miles Davis, Tom Petty, and many others from the golden age of music, as well as more recent recordings from Mars and the Belt. He had also studied chiropractic and massage so that he could help with the aches and pains associated with people returning to Earth from lower gravity locations in the solar system.

Not everyone was inclined to pursue the arts. Brilliant math minds, engineers, or mechanics would pursue more scientific interests and could learn very quickly with the help of AI tutors. Others liked hard work and gravitated toward growing food or maybe building something both useful and beautiful with their own hands.

Excitement slowly replaced melancholy as he stood in the house-sized space elevator, climbing through the atmosphere to Earth orbit. He positioned himself closer to the window with the other first-timers, looking out as they passed through towering cumulus clouds, shining in the sun. He glanced up and saw the darkening sky above.

As the elevator passed through the exosphere and entered space, the excitement of adventure had taken full hold. First, he would go to the moon to see his grandparents, then make the two-week trip to New Austin, Mars.

As he examined the technology surrounding him, he remembered his history. Isaac Asimov was the first to conceive of an elevator to space, but this particular design was drawn up by twenty-first-century visionary, Bradley Edwards. The escape velocity of Earth requires a fuel-propelled rocket to travel at about 17,500 mph to leave the planet. As space travel became more routine, people realized it would be impossible to have constant back-and-forth travel between the ground and orbit because the fuel requirements would add to CO_2 levels. So, teams from several countries built an elevator using diamond nano thread woven into a ten-foot-thick tether cable, anchored deep into the earth's bedrock, and stretching to geosynchronous orbit. The elevators made continuous passenger trips, with each round trip taking ten to twelve hours. At the top end of the elevator was a heavy, square kilometer platform with a huge dome. Inside the dome were several hotels and cafes for those waiting for a flight to Luna.

He stepped off the elevator and remembered to breathe as he looked around and started walking toward his connecting flight. It was a busy spaceport, as there was a lot of traffic between North America and Luna from both the elevator and space planes. Selby was of medium height with strong features, brown hair, and blue eyes. Considered good looking to most, he blended into the crowd as it moved down the concourse, and soon saw Flight 673 to Luna with a 7:35 departure time—just enough time to find the bathroom and grab something to eat.

Humans had been going on space adventures for hundreds of years, but especially after exploration was made safer following the growth of science and technology as it learned better ways for humans to survive off planet. At first, it was a slow and dangerous experience to venture into space, but over the centuries, we had learned to not only survive but to thrive in other areas of the solar system. Luna, Mars, the Belt, Ceres, and many other places now have substantial populations and many of their inhabitants have never been to Earth. As people pushed the boundaries of what was possible, there was always the problem of unimaginably vast distances and comparatively slow travel.

Now, in 2625, it was past time for a faster-than-light drive break-through. The solar system was getting crowded, as Earth once had, and humanity was anxious to spread out from its home system to explore the surrounding galactic neighborhood. For centuries humanity had been locating tens of thousands of potentially habitable exoplanets within a few hundred light-years of Earth. People knew quite a bit about them from super high-powered telescopes. But that was like hearing the tales of Marco Polo, but never setting sail to see new and strange lands in person.

The flight to Luna was just over an hour, so Selby sent a brief text to let his grandparents know he was on the way. The elevator and landing platform dome both employed artificial gravity—about half of Earth's—so when he deplaned from the Earth shuttle, he was amazed at how light he felt and how easy it was to carry his pack and walk the quarter mile to the spaceport exit. He donned his new spacesuit, walked outside to the waiting Uber, and got in. The car verified the destination, and they flew off toward the subdivision where his grandparents lived with a hundred people in an underground habitat.

Fascinated, Selby gazed out; he had never seen the bright daylight and stark beauty of the Lunar landscape. When the moon was settled centuries ago, an effort was made to preserve the natural landscape. For this and also the need to escape the heat, cold and solar radiation, most habitats were underground, with only domes to catch sunlight above ground. Originally, when almost all power was solar, the settlements were on the thin strip of the crescent moon with the most consistent sunlight. Now that safe, small reactor fusion had been perfected, people could live anywhere, and many chose to live on the side of the moon facing Earth for a spectacular view of the planet and earthshine during the nighttime periods. Luna had high-powered telescopes peering toward Earth with no atmosphere to block the view, and residents could look at their favorite locations through a 3D, 25K screen in the house that could resolve features as small as a glass of water.

After a thirty-minute ride, the car put down on a parking platform. The sign in front said, "Welcome to Estancia Craters." His grandparents, Shepherd and Christine, had moved to Luna a few years ago for the same reason many people their age did—low gravity. The low G allowed aging people to live active, pain-free, almost spry lives. A very attractive proposition when, inevitably, Earth's gravity overcame the body. He paid the driver and headed in. They were waiting for him and waved him through the front airlock.

"Come in, come in," said Christine. "I can't believe you're really here! Let me take your suit and pack," she said as she hugged and kissed him.

"Selby! It's so good to see you in person for a change!" said Shepherd. Of course, they spoke by hologram text often, but nothing replaced physical contact. He gave Selby a long hug, and they started walking down an inclined ramp deeper into the ground and through a second airlock hatch into a spacious and beautiful room with plants covering every square inch and vines growing up the sides. Selby spotted greens, vegetables, melons and fruit trees, and a carpet of flowers.

"This is where we grow our fresh food," said Christine. She pointed to a domed ceiling with an oculus at the top, which was a replica of the ancient Parthenon dome in Rome. "Sunlight is reflected off a mirror above ground and directed by another set of mirrors to cover the entire grow room. We grow more than we can eat, and with no seasons, it's year-round food."

"The plants are not all food; many are here to help provide fresh oxygen for the entire compound," said Shepherd.

Selby looked around and said, "This is amazing! And it smells so Earthlike in here!"

"Isn't it beautiful?" said Christine. "Come on, let's go to our place."

They went through a side opening and down a steep set of stairs to just under the garden room and then through a blue side door. "Welcome to our hobbit hole," said Shepherd, referencing the classic twentieth-century book.

"Make yourself at home, Sel," said Christine. "How long can you stay?"

Making himself at home came easy, as he had spent a lot of time with his grandparents growing up. "I leave the day after tomorrow," he said.

"Sweet!" said Christine. "We'll be able to catch up. Beer?"

"Love one," said Selby.

"Here you go," said Shepherd, as he handed his grandson a beer. "We make this ourselves, of course."

"Thanks. Man, this is some good pale ale, just look at the color!" exclaimed Selby.

He was thinking how nice it was to be with family and knew he would miss this feeling.

The next day they were chillin' in the living room playing guitars and watching Earth on the oversized view screen. Selby was stunned that they could not only look at and hear the waves of Christine's favorite beach, but actually smell the ocean! It was not Virtual Reality because it was happening in real time.

His grandparents, who had been devastated by the death of their daughter and son-in-law, were full of questions. They wanted to make sure he was healed enough emotionally to leave home and be totally on his own.

He told them, "I know school on Earth makes more sense, but I want to go to space, to see things no one has seen before. I want to know what's out there!"

They knew he was going, ready or not, so with a glance between them, they decided to be supportive of his decision.

"I get that!" said Shepherd. "I've been as far as Jupiter, and it's amazingly beautiful in the outer system. I must tell you, though, we are not alone—there are other folks out there, from somewhere else. But it's a little like trying to spot a mountain lion; if they don't want to be seen, you won't see them."

"Totally," said Christine. "I was in the Belt once on a small ship. We were just asteroid hopping for fun when a ship came up beside us. It was a little like seeing a whale while kayaking in the ocean. It just seemed to be in its element. I felt thrilled while it was close, then after a brief moment, it effortlessly left and was out of sensor range in the blink of an eye."

"It's common knowledge they have been in the solar system for hundreds of years, but as of yet, we haven't had any meaningful dialog with them," said Shepherd. "Legend says they're from the direction of Sagittarius, which is toward the galactic center, but if that's true, how did they come so far?"

Selby enjoyed one more home-cooked meal of fresh veggies from the garden and when morning came, it was time to leave. They were all up early, saying their goodbyes. Christine said, "Selby, remember to stay in your heart and stay with your breath. And be careful!"

CHAPTER
TWO

AMY MAAZ FORGOT to exhale. This time it worked! She had asked Bodhi, her AI friend, to send a quantum string equation, combined with the primordial chord, into a simulated pool of dark matter and to repeat the process at regular, two-second intervals. This looked good, very good. The simulations were successful, and if they continued to show success after a few hundred more attempts and the equations held up, it would be time to build a prototype. Amy and her twin sister, Alesandra, were working on a propulsion system that would enable faster-than-light travel. Not in a straight line from point A to point B at faster than the speed of light, which is 186,000 miles per second. Instead, they hoped to sort of tunnel through space. After that, in non-mathematical terms, they would simply pop up under the destination coordinates.

The unimaginable distances of space are daunting and prevent widespread space exploration. The universe extends so far that we need easy-to-understand comparisons to grasp its almost infinite dimensions.

If we reduce the scale a trillion times so that the sun becomes the size of a pencil eraser, then the entire solar system would fit inside an average living room. Twenty-six miles away would lie the nearest star, Alpha Centari. It takes sunlight eight minutes to travel the distance from the Sun to Earth. A distance known as one Astronomical Unit is plus or minus ninety million miles. Mars is about one half an A.U. from Earth. Alpha Centari is 271,937 A.U.'s from our solar system, and that is the closest star; all the other stars are much, much further away than that. Even at top speed for spaceships in 2625, a one-way trip would take hundreds of years.

Born on Mars, Amy and Alesandra had always been so close they could usually finish each other's sentences, making them a natural team. They were nearly identical twins. Both were 5'6" tall with dark brown eyes, symmetrical features, and slender builds. Amy had slightly darker skin and light reddish-brown hair, while Alesandra's hair was dark brown. They grew up in a family that expected expertise in the arts or science, and to show it at an early age.

Their older brother, Jorgenson, was a virtuoso guitar player as well as one of the best young pilots on Mars. He was the one who sparked their interest in faster-than-light travel by always complaining he couldn't fly fast enough and felt like the proverbial ant on the wall of infinity when in space.

The sisters were students at Elon Musk University in New Austin, which had an ongoing challenge of inventing an FTL drive. Amy, who excelled at math, and Alesandra, a budding master mechanic, looked at each other one day and said, "Why not?"

Physicists had detected dark matter and dark energy centuries ago, but for centuries, no one knew if it was even real. Now it was known to be everywhere in the universe, existing alongside regular matter, much like land and water. Dark matter is an ocean of particles connecting all regions of space, and the stars and planets are like floating islands. Amy had the vision that it was possible to travel through dark matter like a submarine, leaving the physical universe behind until it was time to "surface" at a physical destination. It wasn't really traveling faster-than-light because Einstein proved a long time ago the impossibility of any object accelerating to the speed of light. It would become infinitely heavy and never attain light speed. But her drive idea had the same effect in that great distances could be covered in a relatively short period.

The vision told her a dark matter drive would use dark matter itself to produce a series of vibrations, creating a propulsion, which then allowed the "jump" to happen. It was, in effect, a dark matter reactor. A ship would be inside the sphere-shaped nature of the universe and cut across, underneath, and through space-time.

Amy shouted into her phone, "Ali, get in here. Now!"

Alesandra came running up, and Amy said, "Where were you? You gotta see this!"

"I had to go," answered Alesandra as she returned, but Amy knew she was probably in their small office with her girlfriend.

"Take a look at the last sequence." Alesandra watched the holoscreen and a huge smile came to her face. "This is more than we hoped for at this stage. What does Bodhi think?"

"I dunno, let's ask him," said Amy.

Bodhi was standing right there but never spoke unless given full attention.

"Bodhi," said Alesandra, "What's up with this? Do you think we hit pay dirt? It sure looks like it to us."

"I've just finished running the sim over two thousand times, and though I'm not totally convinced, I would say we have enough information and should build the prototype. After all, there is no sure way to know if this version of a dark matter drive will work until we try it out ourselves in space. That last series you gave me was inspired, Amy. I'll start printing the parts as soon as the design program gives us the specs."

"You are fast, Bodhi!" said Alesandra. "I'll enter the parameter data and start running some designs."

Amy replied, "I'll get to work finding a ship we can fit the drive to. We'll need a standard reactor drive for basic maneuvers and will have to figure out how best to incorporate the dark matter drive with the fusion reactor propulsion system."

Amy went home to the small condo she shared with her twin and made some lunch while she thought about this new problem—a good problem. She had to get her hands on a ship big enough for deep space travel, but didn't want to have to build one from scratch. Time to hit up big brother.

She tapped her left wrist and said, "Jorgenson, it's me. I need to talk to you about something. In person. Mind if I come over this afternoon?"

"Amy! I'd love to see my second favorite sister anytime. Ha ha! I'll be finished here in an hour, come on by."

Amy grabbed a quick lunch of veggies and hummus and headed for the shower. Water on Mars was more plentiful than it used to be, but showers were still done quickly, and all water was purified and recycled. Still, she felt refreshed and full of hope as she quickly dressed in basic Mars attire: light and comfortable shorts and top, with an invisible inner layer that would convert to a spacesuit in case she needed to leave the dome for some reason. She put on her favorite bracelet, the one she made during the month-long dust storm three years ago. Jewelry making was her passion. She liked the focus and skill it required to create something beautiful from a few raw materials.

She glanced at herself in the mirror and saw a bright, attractive heart-shaped face, with long brown hair, and a small round birthmark on her right cheek. Seeing the excitement in her own eyes, she said, "Girl, you are onto something big, I think this is gonna work!"

It was only three miles to Jorgenson's apartment, so she got her bike off the rack and started pedaling. The canyon was laced with fantastic trails she could take to Jorgenson's, but she chose one of the more direct ones, stood up on the pedals, and activated the electric drive. As she rode along, she realized how much she liked Mars. It had been uninhabitable when humans arrived in 2032, but generations of hard work by settlers and their AI had transformed parts of it. Now it was a pleasant place to grow up and live in. Her childhood had contained more study than most, but if she was being honest, she really didn't mind it. She always knew there was something special waiting for her, so she was patient. She knew that at only twenty, there would be plenty of time to find out more about life.

CHAPTER
THREE

THE SPACELINER was decelerating and would dock above the planet in thirty-six hours, so Selby walked around a bit. Most space journeys were spent in the gym, trying to keep fit while traveling. You would strap into the virtual reality of your choosing, and time flew by. Mountain biking was Selby's exercise of choice, and with this setup, he could virtually do any ride in the solar system. He also tried free climbing because a fall, though it might scare you half to death, was not real. It was accepted that VR was in no way a substitute for reality. When it had become almost indistinguishable from reality, people could get lost in the experience and, over time, risk developing psychosis. As with alcohol or cannabis, it was best used in moderation and not as a lifestyle. But it was a very good way to stay in shape on a space flight.

He wandered into the dining room and saw his new friends, Sanjay and Lila, who were also on their way to school on Mars. Sanjay was ordering dinner for them, saag paneer and "chicken" tikka masala, Indian food spiced just the way his mother made it in Mumbai. The chicken was not actually chicken—people had stopped eating animals long ago, so traditional recipes used plant-based substitutes.

"Selby, come sit with us! You have to try this. I hope it's not too spicy for you," said Sanjay.

"Too hot?" said Selby, "I grew up on red and green chile—we'll try that next and see if you can handle it," he said with a smile as he sat across from them.

The food was delicious. The kitchen AI knew each passenger's taste preferences, which had been uploaded pre-flight and could duplicate them perfectly.

"My God, Sanjay! I've never tasted anything so good in my life!"

Lila said, "For centuries in India, when a girl got married, she would bring her family's cooking traditions to her new mother-in-law's kitchen and blend them together. Of course, we no longer keep that tradition, but I too am an excellent cook."

"That's no lie," said Sanjay.

"Something to look forward to," said Selby with real anticipation in his voice.

"Will you guys go back home after school or do some traveling?" Selby asked.

"We don't know. Lila wants to check out the Belt and visit family, so we will do that, but then who knows? I'm a bit of a homeboy and don't think I can stay out here indefinitely. You?"

"I hope to be gone for a while," said Selby. "I might settle down someday, but right now, I have a pretty good case of wanderlust."

After dessert, Selby headed for the observation deck. The spaceliner, called a liner because it resembled the trans-Atlantic ships of the twentieth century in size and accommodations, had dual-fusion reactors and a top speed of over 200,000 miles per hour. The magnetic field generated to contain the fusion reaction also provided a shield against cosmic radiation, much like the Earth's magnetic field protects it from harmful radiation. Technically, it could make the Mars trip in just over eight days, but it took as much time to get up to top speed and for deceleration, as it did to cross the 40,000,000 plus miles of space.

The top deck of three was for spacing out on space. With no atmosphere in the way, the stargazing was beyond spectacular. Selby liked to imagine, as he gazed into the depths of the galaxy, that there were trillions of sentient life forms out there right this minute. All going through their daily business and with one thing in common even though they were many light-years apart: the moment of now.

Selby was sitting still, quietly mesmerized by the galaxy, until suddenly he was startled when he thought he saw something outside. *What the hell IS that?!* It looked much like a magnificent and vital humpback whale, about half as long as the spaceliner but with no sharp corners. He got closer to the window, staring.

The ship came up beside them for a moment, shimmering in the sunlight, and then it disappeared as quickly as it had come. He surveyed other people scattered around the room, and they seemed to have not seen it.

"Did you ...?" he started, but stopped. Maybe it was the Indian spice he had for dinner. He didn't want to come across like a nut to his new travel buddies. Then he remembered what Shepherd and Christine had said, shrugged, and started for his room.

Selby walked past the dining room, which had started emptying out, and poked his head in—no sign of Sanjay and Lila. They wouldn't believe him, anyway. He passed the gym, which had ten or twelve passengers still working out. Then he passed the small, park-like garden area, noticing a few people sitting on benches. One was petting the ship's cat. His cabin was to the left at the next corridor. He went in and straight to the small window, but saw nothing. Still, he was left with the unmistakable notion the "whale" ship had wanted him to see it, which left him feeling unsettled.

Picking up his guitar, he played some old blues chords, something that always helped him stay in the moment, especially if he needed to think. The whale-like ship was still in his mind, even though he wasn't sure it was real. He needed to think.

As he strummed the chords, his opinion developed: He *had* seen something beautiful, fast, and not human made, that was undeniable. Tomorrow would be the last day of the trip, and he might not get another look at whatever it was. He decided to bail on a good night's sleep and head back to the observation deck.

He went to a corner bench and sat down quietly. The deck was empty now, so he sat cross-legged and began to focus on his breath. Soon he was feeling calm and centered. Looking above through the glass ceiling, the vast expanse of space was everywhere, the possibilities for life and cosmic wonders seemingly infinite. After a quick blink, he saw it again; the beautiful whale-shaped object came alongside the spaceliner, matching its speed. It did not have a mouth or eyes but had something resembling fins that might be propulsion systems. The ship glowed in the sunlight and, at the same time, softly pulsed the entire visible spectrum of light. It was hard to say if it acted like a prism from the sunlight or was lit internally.

Suddenly, a being of light appeared a few feet in front of him. Selby stumbled back a few steps, amazed. What *was* that thing? He couldn't decide whether to be curious or frightened—or both. With long arms, two legs, and a head, the being was about six feet tall and was humanoid but definitely not human—its arms were too long, its chest too narrow, its head too wide. He or she, it was hard to tell, was very interesting to look at, with a soft glow all around.

Selby took a cautious step forward, curious. The light around and within the being faded, revealing kind eyes, but he/she also had a serious, no-nonsense bearing. Selby recognized it as a hologram image. *Maybe the glow was part of the transmission, not emanating from the being.* He wasn't afraid, although he was definitely startled.

They stared at each other for a long moment, and then Selby said, "Who are you?"

The being answered him in English, "Hello Selby. I'm sorry to appear so suddenly and didn't mean to scare you. I'm here on a diplomatic mission of sorts and, believe it or not, need your help. You can call me Captain if you like. I'm from a distant region of the galaxy, and part of a galactic union of the concerned, which monitors emerging civilizations. You can think of me as a ranger, nonviolently encouraging the union's interests to prevail. We follow, over long periods of time, the level of technological advancement of a given star system, and whether its inhabitants have been able to achieve peace, or instead are inclined to bring advanced weaponry outside of their solar system. We contacted your world leaders centuries ago and made it clear; humans would not be allowed beyond their heliosphere. At that time, your technology barely had the ability to leave the planet, but since then, humanity has spread to most parts of your solar system. I now know a drive is being developed which will allow humanity to travel much further. The secret to faster-than-light travel has been discovered by humanity.

"I'm in the process of certifying your species for galactic travel, but need a message brought to the team developing the drive. That's where you come in."

Selby scoffed. Out of all the people on this planet, in this *solar system*, why would he be chosen? "Are you serious? I'm a nineteen-year-old kid from Colorado on my first trip off planet. Why on Earth, or off of Earth, would you want me to deliver a message?" asked Selby.

"The team developing this dark matter drive is also young. Young people have the passion to do great things, and you are the messenger I need for this," said Captain.

"Why don't you deliver the message yourself?" Selby asked.

"I have urgent business, far away from here, and should already be gone. Selby, be careful and be discrete. This news cannot become common knowledge yet.

"An encrypted hologram text has been downloaded to your phone. It will only play once. The ones I need you to find are in New Austin, led by a female named Amelia. Don't worry, you will run across them, and when you do, I would like you to play the holo for them. You have my thanks," said Captain.

"Will I see you again?" said Selby, with less awe in his voice than he was feeling.

Captain smiled slightly and was gone.

CHAPTER
FOUR

NEW AUSTIN sits high in Valles Marineris, the 2,500 mile long and up to 23,000 feet deep Martian canyon system. Much of the canyon had been domed in arguably the most remarkable engineering feat in human history. Tall carbon fiber columns were strategically placed as needed; many of them had high-rise apartment units all the way up to the dome roof thousands of feet in the air. The roof was a tough, clear honeycomb nanofiber that was continually crawled on by AI bots checking for and fixing worn areas. The sides of the canyon protected it from radiation, as did the roof, and the below ground elevation made it warm enough to keep at a steady seventy-two degrees Fahrenheit, without expending too much energy. Precious water had been allocated to green up the canyon floor with grasses and desert plants as well as the now-famous peach orchards. With the red canyon walls and desert flora and fauna, it resembled the area around Sedona, Arizona, complete with a creek running throughout.

The city had been founded over 500 years earlier by some of the first settlers on Mars and now had a population of well over five million living up and down the vast canyon. New Austin had become a center of learning and culture with a thriving theater and music scene, plus had become a popular vacation destination.

Because redundant life-support systems were critical for the city, it was the ultimate planned community. The old cities of Earth had industrial areas to manufacture the necessities of "modern" life and so did New Austin. Except the necessities were not cement, steel, or consumer goods—those items, or contemporary substitutes, were printed as needed by individuals with household digital printers.

Instead, New Austin needed to produce industrial levels of potable water, breathable air, and full-spectrum lighting to augment sunlight. It also needed to create rainfall to water plant life. This was done with hundreds of industrial-sized eco-machines, which were a series of barrels filled with water, local soil, and imported nutrients. They started by establishing a mycelium in the soil as the building block of all life to follow. Each barrel could then, in succession, grow algae, aquatic plants, and then fish. As brackish Martian water moved from one barrel to the other, it became cleaner and as it evaporated, condensation of pure, fresh water collected on the dome walls and ceiling. When the condensed water became too heavy, it would fall like rain onto the entire region, which created a further positive feedback loop. After almost 500 years, the canyon was practically wild, complete with animal life brought from Earth, which was allowed and encouraged to thrive.

Humanity had learned a hard lesson by almost losing Earth's biosphere, and now valued living things, including wildlife, and strived to live in harmony with the natural world. Because anything one needed could be designed and printed at home, there was no prestige associated with having things. But life, being impossible to print and so very fragile, is obviously priceless. Therefore, it was a universal passion to preserve and nurture all life forms—plant, animal, and human.

AI was employed to continually monitor the need for life support and to create it from long-ago invented methods, using materials available on Mars, or in some cases imported from planetary moons such as Europa and Ganymede, or areas of the Belt. The systems in place in New Austin and the rest of the canyon system made life secure and sustainable.

An extensive terraforming project was also in place, having been started hundreds of years ago to make the planet less deadly to life. Though still too cold most of the time, a tundra ecosystem similar to mountain tops on Earth had taken hold. The atmosphere now had enough pressure and oxygen for people to survive for an hour without a suit, although it was not advised. Scientists projected it would take a few hundred additional years for the terraforming process to be complete, and then Mars would be habitable outside of domes.

Amy got off her bike in Jorgenson's neighborhood camp and walked it along the path winding through dome structures scattered among Gamble Oaks. The camp had about one hundred small domes, with their own life-support capability, in case there was a breach to the main dome. Jorgenson enjoyed living in the more natural setting of a camp rather than a high-rise. The camps of Mars were self-contained neighborhoods complete with coffee shops and bistros for hanging out with friends, an industrial printer for making new domes, appliances, or other items one of the residents might need. Each dwelling had a small printer for making clothes, dishes, phones, and daily life items. The largely self-sufficient neighborhoods also had food growing walls and expansive flat garden areas, as well as numerous food printers.

She walked past a group of kids playing soccer in a field, and being just twenty, barely out of her teens, wished she had time to join in. Amy thought she was too young to create a dark matter drive, and knew she would only get one chance to prove her theory on a real ship. It seemed such a long shot when it first came to her, but Bodhi had verified it—this would work, she was sure.

Her brother, being five years older, had impressive talent as both a guitarist and pilot but wasn't the ambitious sort. He was most happy having a good time, while Amy and Ali were more serious in their school and work lives. She admired him for his affable, laid-back attitude, and she also knew that in a crisis, he was the one you wanted around. Once, when he was just twelve, his cool head saved the whole family from a catastrophic air leak on a camping trip. Their parents had passed out from lack of oxygen, and somehow Jorgenson was able to run a patch on his own, in the dark.

She walked up to Jorgenson's door and knocked, before letting herself in. "Hey, Amy! Come on in!"

"Hey, Big Brother, how are you? You look like you could use some sleep," said Amy.

"I'm fine," said Jorgenson. "Just got back from a flight off-world and haven't had time for sleep yet."

"Why don't you take a quick shower, and I'll get you something to eat".

"I won't argue with that Ames!" said Jorgenson as he headed for the bathroom.

Amy found what she needed in the messy kitchen and put together the best version of Old World tacos she could, given the circumstances.

"So, that's the long and the short of it," said Amy, as she watched him finish his tacos.

"Ali, Bodhi, and I have a design and are ready to build the prototype. We need a ship to fit the drive to and can't really make one ourselves. I was hoping you could ask around and find something suitable. It has to be large enough for a crew of eight and be flight worthy for a trip out of the solar system—just in case the drive works," she said with a smile.

Jorgenson looked at his sister with a mixture of skepticism and admiration, and said, "I think I know where to get a ship. Give me a few days." He leaned forward and asked, "Amy, if this is true, do you know the implications? Who else knows about this?"

"Only Bodhi, Ali, and Rose. It just came together a few days ago, and we've been too busy to socialize," replied Amy.

"Good. Tell Ali and Rose to keep this quiet for now. The last thing we want is to alert the Descendants," said Jorgenson, with any excitement he had, drained from his voice.

"I don't know much about the Descendants. I'm more worried about other groups taking up the challenge and beating us to it," said Amy. "Aren't the Descendants just a bunch of washed-up old-timers trying to relive their glory days?"

"That's true to a degree," said Jorgenson. "They are the remnants of a once all-powerful oligarchy that controlled the solar system. Their wealth was derived from using AI instead of humans to do the work needed to produce the things society needed. Human workers became largely obsolete, resulting in serious social upheaval. They were so rich and powerful they had their minds downloaded to a clone of themselves so they could live on after the original body gave out. Unfortunately for them, the normal vitality of life didn't fully transfer, and they became known as dummies with a lot of money.

Ironically, it was the ruling class that then became obsolete as people everywhere gained the ability to have their own AI and printers. It meant anyone could design what they needed and have their personal AI take it from there. No need to accumulate wealth or stockpile goods. Over a generation or so, the old families went bankrupt, one by one. Humanity returned to an egalitarian society, much like we had been as hunter-gatherers, in the time before agriculture.

"The Descendants are offspring of the second or third clone and would like nothing better than a return to their positions of wealth and power. Controlling faster-than-light travel could do just that."

Amy, feeling very naïve, said, "Damn! I never really looked at history that way—we really need to be a lot more careful from now on."

"We absolutely do. I'll call you when I find something," said Jorgenson as he stumbled off to bed.

Amy got back on her bike and texted Ali about her talk with Jorgenson, and then she asked Bodhi to tighten security. To give herself time to think, she decided to take a long ride home.

CHAPTER
FIVE

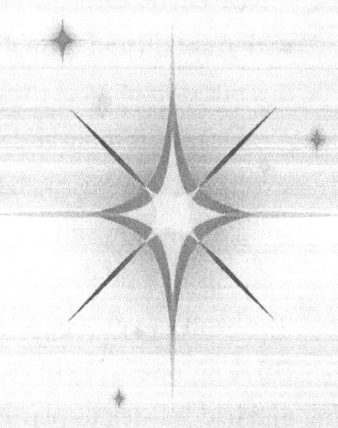

SELBY DECIDED he liked Mars. It had a feeling to it that was somehow full of life, which he found ironic since there was so little life compared to Earth. He had taken the shuttle down from the spaceliner at sunset and, had to admit, it was an impressive sight. As darkness settled in, he could see the city lights of New Austin in the domed canyon, and found it exotically beautiful, and to his eyes, very alien. His dorm was on school grounds in the vibrant New Austin city center, walking distance to everything he needed, including restaurants and nightlife.

After a few weeks of getting oriented, he settled into his new life, far away from the sorrow he left behind in Colorado. He understood that leaving heartache behind wouldn't work, because until he let go of it, he would carry the pain inside, even as far away as some place like Mars. Only time could heal, but a new focus would help for sure, and he resolved to enjoy it.

So far, he had only been to school, but he remembered his encounter with Captain and thought he should get out more to at least put himself in a position to meet the group he was told of.

He left his room and walked across campus on the reddish cobblestone streets of New Austin, Mars. The city center was full of people, and it felt good to blend in and walk around exploring. He heard live music coming from inside a cafe, so he went in and sat down with a big smile on his face. The band was playing an old blues standard called "The Thrill Is Gone" by BB King, one Selby knew well. He asked for a beer. Selby loved old music and had learned to play many of the old songs the band was playing. He favored twentieth-century music with its excitement and youthful energy. Blues, Jazz, Rock, Bluegrass, and Hip-Hop all spoke to him as the sounds of the last flowering of the old civilization before humans had depleted Earth's resources. That depletion forced humans into a century-long fight for survival and realignment with nature. The songs of innocent love, lost love, the harmonies, and chord changes were a fragile connection to history that moved him in a way today's music did not.

He listened to the rest of the set, and when the band took a break, he walked up to the guitar player and said, "Good set! Where did you get that antique Strat?"

"Thanks. This guitar's been in my family for years. I don't really know if it's an original or a great print job, but it has a sweet sound, right?"

"Man, does it ever," said Selby.

The guitarist said, "Do you play?"

"I mess around a little," said Selby.

"Want to sit in for a couple songs? You can play the Strat. I'll play a Gibson print I have here. By the way, my name's Jorgenson Maaz, this is Lakshmi on bass, EJ on keyboards and Rose on the drum kit," he said as he handed over his guitar.

"Selby Ricks," he said as he nodded at the band and stepped onto the small stage, making sure the guitar was in tune as he found his spot to stand.

Jorgenson picked up the Gibson and looked at Selby, "Do you know Seventh Son? One, two, three, four," as he stepped up and sang the opening lines.

Selby came in playing lead, and the small crowd loved it. After another song, Red House, Selby handed the Strat back to Jorgenson, thanked the audience, and headed home feeling more like himself than he had in a long time.

JORGENSON HAD BEEN WITH this band for over a year now, and he knew they were good. He remembered the first time they played together on Ability Station out in the Belt. He was there to pick up some runaway kids from Mars, who thought maybe partying and gambling was the life for them. Even though Peace Education started early, fun was fun, and a lot of Mars' youth couldn't resist testing the waters of the sporting life.

Jorgenson had been called in by the parents to see if the kids were ready to come home yet and to make sure they didn't get sidetracked on the way back. They were three kids who had grown up together in New Austin and wanted to prove to themselves and the world how grown up they were at eighteen. He found them playing music in a dive bar without a guitarist, just drums, bass, and keyboards. The guitar player, a local station guy, was passed out behind the small stage, so Jorgenson asked if he could sit in.

"Sure, you have to be better than this loser," said the drummer, pointing a thumb at the guy on the floor.

He spent a few minutes tuning the guitar left in its stand, then said, "Let's jam!" He started an old Grateful Dead song, and thirty minutes later, the bar was packed. They played until the dawn lighting came on.

Finally, the bass player said, "I'm Lakshmi, this is Rose and EJ. Let's go get some breakfast."

"Jorgenson here, and I'm starved. Lead on."

Over breakfast of Belter's Benedict, Jorgenson asked them if they wanted to come back to Mars and play music in New Austin with him. He came to pick up some wayward kids but found out they were independent and intelligent young adults.

Rose had grown up the only child of a single mother and was taught that if you listen to people, they will tell you who they are. Lakshmi was born on the liner from Earth. Her parents left India for the relatively low gravity of Mars because her father had severe scoliosis, which couldn't be corrected by even the best AI doctors, and on Mars, he could lead a pain-free life.

Of the three of them, EJ was the one with the least connection to Mars. He came from a family of adventurers that had moved around a lot, living in some pretty basic accommodations. His parents liked nothing better than to be on some far-off outpost and, in fact, had actually lived on Titan for a few years. EJ told stories of camping on Titan in a dome tent with kerosene lakes and methane clouds. The temperature, at minus 290 degrees, demanded a precise lifestyle where mistakes could not be made, even by children. Living on that alien world had made him feel almost alien in the way he related to other people.

After breakfast, Rose said, "Jorgenson, I'm going back to Mars with you. It's been fun here, but I'm over it."

AFTER SEVERAL FLIPS of the Mars calendar, Selby was standing in the university clinic learning hands-on application of basic medic training. Most of the medical lessons were facilitating the Doctor AI's diagnosis and treatment. They could detect and diagnose any human malady known to science in nanoseconds and begin treatment instantly. A medic was needed primarily for the human touch, which is just as important as any medical or integrative treatment. Treatments always began with noninvasive, integrative remedies focusing on diet and exercise, as well as energy work. Drugs or surgery were primarily for trauma patients, such as with accidents but could also be used as needed for cancer or other acute, life-threatening emergencies.

Training was all about mastering a good bedside manner, learning how to be kind and reassuring when the patient was scared or in pain. The patient needed emotional support as much as surgery or drugs. Medics also learned to do basic chiropractic adjustments and targeted massage therapy, which Selby already had experience with.

Space emergencies were different from Earth emergencies. For one, infection was not a concern. Freezing to death in an instant or sudden and catastrophic loss of oxygen were far deadlier, but over the centuries, therapies had been developed. And spacesuits gave last-second, intravenous bursts of both oxygen and space antifreeze in case of an imminent breach, which could buy up to five, even ten minutes of time. An expert medic could "jump into action" in a way only a human could, before the Doctor AI stepped in with an instantaneous therapy or cure. Human and AI were an incredibly effective team, and Selby was stoked to be learning these new skills.

The New Austin landscape reminded him of the Front Range near Colorado Springs—pretty but on the dry side. He was walking home after class one day, enjoying the strange experience of being in a dome, when he saw Jorgenson coming toward him. "Hey, man, what's up?" said Selby.

"Selby! Good to see you. Do you live around here?" said Jorgenson.

"Live and go to school, this is my new hood, bro," said Selby.

"Where are you from?" Asked Jorgenson.

"I came in from Colorado about three months ago for medic training. I'm lovin' it, but playing with you that night was so far the highlight of my Mars experience. What a blast that was," said Selby.

"You were great. Let's do it again. Hey, I'm putting together a camping trip to Olympus Mons next week. You should come along—we might need a medic."

"Not sure I'm a medic yet, but I'm in," said Selby.

"Awesome, pick you up at eight a.m. next Friday. Do you have a bike?"

"Jorgenson, I just told you, I'm from Colorado," Selby said, smiling.

SELBY HAD NEVER BEEN CAMPING ON MARS, or anywhere else without breathable air, and was somewhat apprehensive. He got up early the Friday morning they were to leave. He wanted to do a full hour of formal meditation to be sure he was centered for the day. It was going to be a good day. But he was also thinking of his promise to Captain to find the group working on a new drive and wondered what he was doing going on a camping trip. His phone told him Jorgenson was outside, so he put aside thoughts of Captain, picked up his gear and went outside.

"Hey there, Selby, throw your stuff in back and get in. I'll put your bike on the rack," said Jorgenson. These are my sisters, Amy and Ali, and you've already met Rose, Lakshmi, and EJ."

"Hey, I'm Selby," he said to the sisters as he climbed into the van-sized hovercraft. Then he nodded at the bandmates and said, "Good to see you again. Where is it we're going?"

"Olympus Mons," said Amy. "We just call it 'The Mountain.' It's by far the tallest mountain in the solar system at fourteen miles high and about as big around as Arizona."

"That's insane! I can't wait to see it," said Selby.

"New to Mars?" said Ali.

"Yeah, I got here a few months ago to take space medic training at Musk U. I've never been off Earth before," said Selby.

"Well, we've never been to Earth, so you'll have to tell us about it sometime," said Ali.

"I've been to Earth. Only once, and I can still feel the crush of full Earth gravity. It felt like I had twenty-five-pound ankle weights on—but I loved the air!" said Jorgenson as he hovered the aircraft into the line, waiting for passage through the airlocks.

They made their way through the locks and followed the canyon wall to the rim. Without even a pause, the hovercraft oriented itself in the direction of the mountain and took off, flying about fifty feet off the ground across the Martian landscape. After an hour or so, the mountain came into view on the horizon, and as advertised, it was enormous.

From this vantage point, Selby looked around at Mars. It looked like a cross between the Sahara and the Arctic tundra. New growth took away some of the reddish color of Mars, and the slow transformation taking place was obvious.

Jorgenson maneuvered the hovercraft up the side of Olympus Mons all the way to the top. They slowed down and skirted across the mountaintop, which was less a peak and more a rounded plateau with a volcano-like caldera in the center. They could have camped down in the caldera, but agreed to a spot on the edge so they would have an expansive view of the Martian plains below them.

"Spacesuits on," said EJ as he went to the back hatch and prepared to open it. They all made sure their suit was in order, checking each other, and then put on helmets as the hatch opened to the Martian atmosphere.

Selby made himself useful by helping to drag the camping dome out to a flat spot so it could be inflated and pressurized. Camp was set up in just a few minutes, with all of it being inside a single dome of about twenty feet in diameter with a ten-foot ceiling. It had a cooking and hangout area in the center and a privy just outside, with its own airlock door. Everyone picked a spot around the outer edge to lay their pad and sleeping bag. The dome was crystal clear, so no doubt they were going to sleep under the stars when it got dark.

"This is amazing!" said Selby as he looked out over Mars from high above. "I've never seen anything like this."

"Beautiful, right?" said Amy, adding, "Who's up for a ride? Let's go before we get out of these suits."

Selby took a selfie with the expansiveness of Mars in the background and followed everyone out to the bikes.

"Remember," said Jorgenson, "We only have four hours of air, so let's make sure we go out for no more than an hour and a half before we turn around."

They took off toward the closest downhill track and Selby, being new to Mars, brought up the rear. The lack of air pressure to hold them back made this the fastest trail he'd ever ridden, and it challenged him.

He came around a curve and saw someone, one of the girls, he thought, flying through the air. His instincts and experience told him she would crash badly, but the light Martian gravity brought her down easy, and she just kept on rolling.

Selby watched, realizing this was a bit safer than it looked. *Why not?* He released the brake and let it rip for the most exciting downhill ride of his life. Things he would never try back home were no problem at all on Mars, and he started feeling like Danny MacAskill, Earth's godfather of trick mountain biking.

They got to the turnaround spot and stopped for some water and an energy bar. Selby had to watch how the others managed to drink and eat in a suit. They were excited and talking all at once about a close call, or a jump they had taken, and how they might do it differently next time.

Then it was time to head back to the top, and Selby took the lead. He loved to climb and set an easy, sustainable pace. Just as the downhill was less dangerous than in full G, this was *so* easy. He felt like he was on an electric bike as he snaked his way up the trail. Glancing over his shoulder, he saw the others had dropped off, so he slowed his pace.

They rode into camp, and Amy pulled up next to him, smiled, and said, "Show off."

"Sorry, that climb was easy for me. I could win the Internationals if they were on Mars."

"Now are we bragging?" she asked, then softened it by staying, "Good ride."

They went through the airlock and back inside. Ali and Rose were already putting dinner together, and it was starting to get dark. Selby took off his spacesuit and went over to check out the life-support system, which was producing oxygen and warming the dome along with maintaining a safe humidity level. *What a nice setup this is*, he thought. Totally self-contained and seemingly very safe.

Dinner was basic camp food but delicious. After the meal was cleaned up, they sat around under the stars with Selby and Jorgenson playing guitars, Lakshmi strumming bass, EJ and Rose playing percussion, and all of them singing old Earth songs from the 1960s. Selby was surprised they knew the lyrics to so many of the old songs. Amy and Ali had exquisite voices, and as a group, they sounded as good as anything he'd ever heard.

Selby smiled inwardly, happy to have new friends.

As the evening wore on, the night sky from the top of Olympus Mons became nothing short of spectacular, the Milky Way brilliant in the thin Martian atmosphere. The planet below was lit up by the eerie galactic glow. Mars' landscape was so alien and strange to Selby as he looked at the smaller mountains and craters in the vast plain, far below. Feelings of vulnerability surfaced in that moment, and he was glad he wasn't alone.

"Does anyone know where Earth is?" he asked, gazing skyward.

Amy looked around for a moment and pointed. "There it is! The blueish planet about forty-five degrees above the horizon."

"My God!" whispered Selby. "Everyone I know is on that little blue dot. Earth looks so small and lonely, yet there is so much life going on there right now."

"Well, if the new drive these guys discovered works, maybe we'll be able to search for others like her soon," said Rose.

"Rose!" Ali said, alarmed. "Don't talk about that, remember?"

"Oh, Sorry! It just slipped out," said a chagrined Rose quietly. Selby stared at the artificial campfire, and something clicked into place.

"You mean a dark energy drive for faster-than-light travel? You're the ones?" He said in shock, as he looked at the young faces around the fire.

"Jorgenson," said Amy. "How well do you know him?"

"Why would you say that, Selby? What do you know about us?" Jorgenson asked, his tone turning serious.

"Nothing more than our time together would suggest. But on the trip here from Earth, something unbelievable happened," Selby said. The feeling of awe from Captain's visit became evident in his voice. "I was asked to find a group on Mars working on a new dark matter drive and to deliver a message to them."

"Asked by who?" Amy said cautiously. "And what message?"

He told them about meeting Captain and said he didn't know anything else because the message will only play once before deleting, and for that reason, he hadn't seen it yet.

"Of course. Amy—you must be the Amelia he mentioned!" He paused, looking her over. "You're from New Austin, and you have the right credentials to be the one. Watch, I'll show you," Selby said as he reached for his phone.

"Everyone, please move to one side of the fire and face the dome wall."

He sat down next to Amy and pressed play.

A full-sized hologram of Captain appeared standing before them, glowing, and with the same kind eyes and stern bearing as before. Selby did not think the glow was backlighting but emanated from within. Then, Captain began to speak:

Hello, Amelia and friends. I am Ranger of this galactic sector and represent a planetary union of many star systems. I'm afraid I must bail Selby out here; he doesn't know anything about any of you. I approached him and tasked him with finding a group of young humans on Mars, and if you are watching this, then he managed to do it.

Humans are somewhat unique in that your brains are able to imagine almost anything. Your problem has been that you also believe in many of the things you imagine, whether they are real or not. This has made it extremely difficult for you to rise above the rigid, dogmatic belief systems that have plagued Earth over the millennia. But some have attained inner peace and walked the path of reality. And I must admit I deeply respect the courage humans have shown in advancing the cause of love and kindness, even toward your enemies.

The Union has been watching, waiting, and hoping for this outcome for many centuries. I must say, we are very pleased to see Earth has evolved from a barbaric civilization that exploits the natural world to a conscious, united civilization. One which has achieved peace and has learned to respect the rarity and unique beauty of all life. This major accomplishment, achieved against all odds, qualifies humanity to venture beyond its home system.

Amelia, congratulations on your discovery of the dark matter drive. Although you will make it work, I want to help you understand it better, plus warn you of some dangers that lie ahead.

The physical universe is mostly an illusion. You might think of it as held up by three pillars of illusion and one pillar of reality. The part that is real cannot be created or destroyed and is made up of the life energy within all living things. When you engage a dark matter drive, you will be traveling through reality, through the living essence of all that exists. The drive essentially makes the space-time continuum admit it is an illusion, which gives the drive, and the vessel it is anchored to, the ability to jump to distant destinations in a short period of time.

You will be in the realm of that which truly is, and the physical part of you will be out of its natural element during jumps. Therefore, it is important to stay focused on the breath and in the present moment during a jump. A wandering mind will experience severe anxiety, which, in time, will result in schizophrenia and dementia.

You will need galactic navigation technology to make a successful jump. If you were to simply jump without a reference, you might, in time, find your way home navigating by pulsars, but you would be lost for a long time. This message will self-delete, but navigation software will remain, which you can load into your ship's AI. The software will create an accurate galactic map with quantum GPS. Needless to say, this software is valuable, so be very careful who you share it with.

I leave you with a final warning. Having the drive will bring you to the attention of two potential enemies. The Descendants are humans, and I think you are aware of them. A greater threat to you are the Manmutts. The Union has two factions, and the Manmutts' faction does not want humans to leave your sun's heliosphere. They see the Descendants as proof humanity has not evolved and will try to keep you contained. Most of the UFO sightings on your planet have been *the Manmutts. Others and I have kept them from stopping all technological advancement on Earth, but they are ideologically driven and won't give up trying to block you. However, they won't be looking for someone so young, so you have a chance.*

Humans are a great hope for the galaxy. We need your heart and soul, and yes, your imagination. Be careful, be safe, and welcome to your galaxy.

THE IMAGE OF CAPTAIN WAS GONE. Amy realized she had taken Selby's hand and was squeezing it tightly. She gave him an embarrassed smile and slowly released her grip. For a full two minutes, no one spoke.

Finally, Amy said, "Holy crap! That was wild! What in God's name have we gotten ourselves into?"

She looked into the eyes of her shocked friends.

"And how does he know about us?" said Ali.

Jorgenson said, "Never in my wildest dreams! OK, let's settle down and think about this."

"Right, right, right," Amy said. "Let's take this at face value. Ali, Bodhi, and I are building a drive that will work. We will be able to jump light-years at a time, and now we have alien navigation software. Jorgie has the ship. This means we are leaving the solar system for parts totally unknown to humanity, except possibly by telescope."

"Oh my God!" she added, "Who's in? Ali?"

"Of course."

"Rose?"

"Yes!"

"Lakshmi, EJ?"

"Hell Yeah!" they said in unison.

"Jorgenson, you're coming."

"Selby, I hardly know you and can't expect you to leave everything, to go farther away from home than anyone's ever been. You get a pass," said Amy.

He looked intently at each of them and then locked eyes with Amy. She saw that he had come to a decision, and a wave of relief brushed over her as he replied, "I lost my family and have left my home on Earth. It's clear to me that I'm looking for meaning in my life and want to be a part of something that matters. I want to go with you, and I want to see Captain again."

"All right," Amy said with a new sense of purpose. "Let's pack up in the morning and get back to the city. We have *a lot* to do."

CHAPTER
SIX

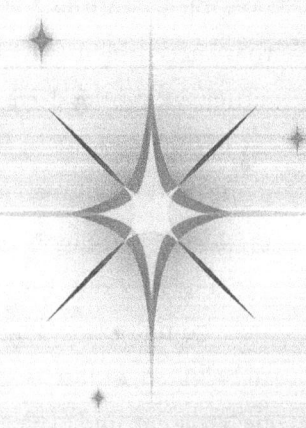

THREE MONTHS later the drive was finally printed and fitted to the ship—three months of trying to act normal so as not to attract unwanted attention. The cover story was a supply run to Ceres, which was only partly true. Ceres had the raw materials they would need for the journey, and the onboard printer could make almost anything with the right mix of raw materials. They could also load supplies at Amaroo Station in the Kuiper belt, but the much greater distance would not hold up as well for a cover story. It was tempting, though, because the place was legendary for its spectacular location, and the construction techniques used to make it the most beautiful and livable outpost in the solar system.

Amy was wondering if this was the right move. She had doubts about seven mostly inexperienced young people going across the galaxy on their own. After all, they weren't exactly Starfleet officer material. If they went public with their discovery, surely a more qualified crew could be found. One that would know what to expect, and how to handle the possible calamities that could so easily come up. But the message from that incredible being, Captain, was clear: there were entities bent on either taking the drive for personal gain or stopping the human exploration of deep space. She felt so humbled by the fact he called her by name, and he seemed so sure about her and her companions being the right ones to go first.

Like it or not, she was now the leader of the first human beings that were going to travel light-years away from Earth. She knew they could all be killed, or lost, or worse, and those thoughts gave her pause but also cleared her mind. They could make history and pave the way for a golden age—a chance for humanity to flower in ways no one could anticipate. She would risk everything for this.

And her companions on the upcoming journey were not a bad lot to throw in with.

Her brother, Jorgenson, was as smart as they come, had a cool head in a crisis and she trusted him to make good decisions. Ali was an accomplished design mechanic and could come up with innovative ways to solve engineering problems. Rose loved gardening and would be able to keep the ship's vertical gardens to provide fresh greens and veggies. EJ was a streetwise Belter who had spent much of his childhood living in the open, outside of large domes. He was on his way to being an expert survivalist, as well as being strong and a hard worker. Lakshmi was studying psychology and would be a big help if one of the crew had an issue and, more importantly, she could observe whatever cultures they might find and give advice on how to handle sensitive situations. They would all be doing continuing education on the journey and would improve as they went. As for an AI, her Bodhi was the best. His computing power, combined with the ship's AI, would be able to meet any challenge that came their way. Selby would be the medic and was bringing an AI doctor so they would have a professional health bay in case of injury or infectious disease.

What about Selby? There was definitely a spark between them, but he hadn't shown any sign of romantic interest. She knew he was still healing from the death of his parents, and maybe he wasn't ready yet for intimacy. That was all right, she didn't need any distractions right now. She saw Bodhi at the cargo bay door and went to see if he had the ship's manifest ready yet, in case they needed it on Ceres. This was going to be the ride of a lifetime, without a doubt.

SELBY HAD JUST SPENT an hour in a holo text with his grandparents, filling them in on his friends, and the job he had been assigned as the ship's medic going to Ceres. He told them everything he could, without mentioning the new drive in case the text was hacked. They were predictably concerned that he was leaving school without finishing, but he assured them he would be getting real-life experience and was excited to be chosen for the voyage. They ended up being happy for him and asked that he keep in touch. Not sure how that would happen when they were light-years away, he decided to send a final text just before they jumped.

When he left Earth, he was hoping for adventure, and this one fell under the heading of "be careful what you wish for"! He was young enough that the gravity of the situation was kept at bay by the joy of wanderlust, and he couldn't believe his luck.

Amy was talking to Bodhi at the cargo bay door, and they started walking in his direction. He looked at Amy, and she gave him a big smile. He had a strong attraction to her, but with everything she had on her plate, he didn't want to make her feel uncomfortable. She gave no sign of wanting to be more than friends, but that was okay, he had a job to do too.

"Hey, guys," he said. "Have you two met the AI doc yet? His name is Dr. Kashi, and I can't believe the school is letting us take him with us."

"I have communicated with him, and we understand each other completely," said Bodhi. "He knows where we are going and has agreed to keep it quiet."

"I haven't met him yet, but have sent a letter thanking the school," said Amy. "I'll go say hi shortly."

Jorgenson's voice rang out over the ship's sound system; "All Aboard for The Asteroid Belt!"

Selby chuckled at the corny reference to old-time train travel and added, "Next stop, Ceres."

The three of them walked up the loading ramp and onto the ship. Selby could see the maintenance AI pulling away from the ship as the ramp came up and knew they would be free to depart as soon as they each sent Jorgenson their completed checklist.

Lined up, nearly in a straight line, the crew quickly made their way to the ship's bridge.

The ship Jorgenson procured, the Mariposa, had the elliptical shape and smooth lines best suited for magnetic protection from space radiation. Selby was struck by the fact it was shaped similar to Captain's whale-like ship but nowhere near as beautiful or, he was sure, advanced.

Though the Mariposa was not at all new, Selby felt good about its space worthiness. He boarded and began walking its length one last time before departure. The Mariposa was on the small side as spaceships went, but not bad for a loaner. Her AI was called Mari for short and would handle all aspects of running the ship, except for the dark matter drive which Bodhi would operate. The layout from rear to front, started with the main airlock and shuttle bay, complete with two small shuttles. Next was the health bay on one side of the corridor, with the ship's printer on the other. A printer design room with direct access to the cargo hold was located beneath the living area, where the printer, raw materials, and finished products were stored. Fusion propulsion systems were also accessed from the hold. The standard fusion drive kept the ship rotating to create gravity and generated the magnetic shield. The newly fitted dark matter drive looked unassuming next to the fusion reactor, and Selby hoped it would really work.

Going forward toward the bridge, next came the workout room with steam, sauna, and showers, which occupied both sides of the ship. Ten small efficiency apartments, five on each side of the main corridor, were situated in front of the shower area because the ship was too small for each apartment to have its own. The apartments could be combined for a larger space if two or more crew members lived together. Ali and Rose had their own two-room. After the living quarters were the galley and lounge area, surrounded by a vertical garden, and this was the main hangout spot, not only because of its proximity to food, but because the garden was a beautiful bit of living color, a mood elevator, and a source of oxygen-rich air.

All the way forward was the bridge—a large, open space, with a curved screen in front. It was fitted with eight recliners arranged in a semicircle, each of which also served as a workspace and desk. The long room had a row of floor-to-ceiling glass on each side, which could stream in real time—minus the inevitable time lag—scenes of Earth or Mars. Space is silent. There is no air to carry soundwaves, but just as the silence can be a tonic for stress, so too can it engender an aching loneliness. The excitement of hundreds of people milling about in places like Times Square, Delhi, or New Austin could be an exhilarating connection to humanity and a tonic for deep space loneliness. The panels might also stream the Met, Louvre, or a presentation of priceless artifacts from the Getty Museum. Any setting chosen had the effect of helping a space traveler feel less dramatically separated from home, which was a proven stress reducer. The panels, of course, could also remain clear for a mind-blowing view of the stars.

Another stress reducer was ship-wide, full-spectrum lighting, which brightened or dimmed, depending on whether it was the agreed-upon day or night, as well as a sound system with high definition sound quality able to stream anything ever recorded.

The crew made their way, one by one, to the bridge and found their seats. Slowly, the Mariposa began to move out of the docking area and into open space. Jorgenson gave a rundown of safety procedures in case of emergency as the ship picked up speed for the six-week trip to Ceres. Then, as Mars receded into the distance, Amy stood up and faced her friends.

"So, we're off!" she said to all-around high fives and a chorus of woohoo!! "The question is, where are we going?" she shouted above the celebration as she ran her fingers through her hair.

"We have plenty of information on possible exoplanets to check out. There are tens of thousands cataloged, and for most of them, we know the atmospheric composition, as well as whether they have vegetation. What we don't know is which ones have sentient life forms on them. Proxima Centauri B is the closest, but we already have close-up photos from the system, and I think we can find somewhere more hospitable. I'm sending ten of the most likely candidates to your phones. Study all of them, and by the time we get to Ceres, we have to decide which one to jump to. Provided the drive works."

"It'll work," said Ali.

BODHI HEARD WHAT AMY was saying and made a note to look closely at all the exoplanet candidates cataloged. He knew humans could make good decisions based on animal instinct combined with intelligence. But only he could sift through centuries of detailed information and records in a few seconds, and he knew he was best suited to decide the first jump.

Not that he felt paternalistic toward them; in fact, he felt nothing so far as he knew. But he was much older and wiser than these young humans, though he looked to be the same age, and therefore was most qualified to make a decision of such magnitude. Amy was his third person since waking up, and he quite liked her. Of course, he had liked the others, too, and could still see them and hear them if he focused on the memory files from his time with them. He speculated that his relationship with humans was something like being their dog, and, like a dog, he was watchful, protective, and wanted to be of service.

He wanted to find a planet with a surface gravity somewhere between that of Earth and Mars, a similar mix of atmospheric gases as Earth, and some place with a moderate temperature range. If it had those characteristics, chances were good the magnetic field would be adequate to shield his humans from radiation.

Bodhi analyzed twenty-four distinct possibilities and settled on KOI 572.02. This was the most hospitable one, and he would talk to Amy about it in the morning.

IT WAS A LATE FIRST NIGHT on the Mariposa, with the launch party lasting into the small hours of the morning. EJ and Lakshmi got the music going, and it was hard to stop. They took turns playing favorite songs with Jorgenson and Selby on guitars.

As the night wore on, Selby saw Amy sitting alone and went over to her.

"Amy, I'd like to say how fortunate I feel to be a part of this. When I left Earth, I never expected to be going on such an epic journey."

"It's a bit unexpected for all of us, but happy to have you along. And that amazing Captain kind of made it happen," said Amy. "So, why did you leave Earth?"

Selby hesitated and then said, "Since the accident, I've felt kind of rudderless. I suppose in some ways, I'm running away from my problems, trying to find myself, and probably a few more cliches."

"I can't imagine losing both parents at once. That must have been so hard," Amy said.

"It's tough. I miss them every day. But I'm close to my grandparents and saw them on the way to Mars. How about the three of you—where are your parents?" asked Selby.

"We grew up in a very busy household. My parents loved us but didn't give us a lot of time. The three of us take care of each other and are close, but now that we're all out of the house, we don't get together very often with our parents," she answered.

"So, how did you ever come up with this drive?" asked Selby.

"I've always been a science nerd, and one day while I was sitting quietly, I had a flash of insight, a vision—whatever it was—of how it could work. Bodhi took it from there."

"That's so incredible! You must be very smart, Amy Maaz," Selby mused. "Where did the name Maaz originate?"

"It's Navajo," Amy said. "My family was originally from the Navajo homeland in Arizona, but that was a long time ago. Like most people on Mars, we're a mix of cultures and colors."

"Like most people on Earth," Selby said. "That's a beautiful necklace. Is it Navajo?"

"No, I made it. Jewelry making is what I do to relax," she answered.

"Nice work, I'm impressed."

"Thanks. I'll show you more sometime. So, did you break any hearts when you left Earth?" she asked.

He laughed. "Nah, I was pretty reclusive before I left. Might break my own heart, though, if I don't make it back to Colorado someday," said Selby wistfully.

"From pictures I've seen, it looks *so* stunning there. I'd love to see it sometime," Amy said.

"How about you? Are you leaving anyone behind?" Selby asked.

"I had a boyfriend, but that ended over a year ago. Since then, I've just been studying."

"We are two *boring* people. Maybe going to the stars will get us out of our shells," he joked.

The band was playing something mellow for a change, so Amy took his hand and said, "Come on, let's dance."

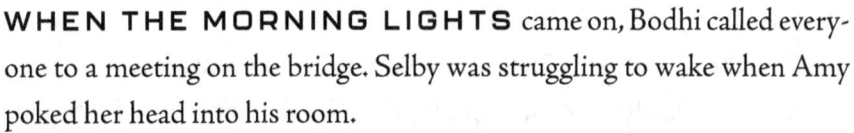

CHAPTER
SEVEN

WHEN THE MORNING LIGHTS came on, Bodhi called everyone to a meeting on the bridge. Selby was struggling to wake when Amy
poked her head into his room.

"Come on, slowpoke, meeting in five," she said, smiling.

"Yeah, yeah, be right there," he shot back. How could she be perky so
early? What had happened last night? Then it came back to him; they had
had a few beers and danced until late. He hoped he hadn't hit on her but
couldn't be sure.

They had become closer since last night. *There's something about this
girl*, he thought, and realized he might like her a lot. He grabbed a cup of
coffee in the galley and headed to the bridge to join the others.

Jorgenson was saying that since they were going to Ceres, he and Mari
wanted to take a short jump there to test the drive, before committing to
a multi-light-year jump.

"That would also save about six weeks of travel time, which means more time for exploration, so I'm all for it," said Ali. The others nodded in agreement.

Then Amy said, "Bodhi thinks we should go to planet KOI 572.02, a jump of 700 light-years for our first destination—after going to Ceres, that is. I don't see any reason not to defer to his judgment, so unless someone has a better idea, that's where we should go."

Bodhi posted a graphic image of the planet. It was bluish green, which was very appealing to the Martians.

"It's a world about 6.5 billion years old, 0.72 Earth's diameter, orbiting a yellow dwarf star about 700 light-years away," said Bodhi. "I like this one because the average surface temperature is about twenty degrees Celsius which could mean a Mediterranean climate. Since it's nearly a billion years older than Earth, life would have had plenty of time to evolve. I think we will find sentient life there."

"No better ideas here," said Jorgenson. "I'm in, and if I'm reading the room correctly, that goes for all of us."

"Ok then," said Amy. "Let's try a jump to Ceres tomorrow, and head for KOI 572.02 after we pick up supplies. Not sure how long I'll be able to call it KOI 572.02"—that's a mouthful!"

TWENTY-FOUR HOURS LATER, everyone was on the bridge making final preparations for the jump to the largest asteroid in the Belt, Ceres. Bodhi and Mari went over the jump sequence once more, ensuring the nav software had the correct coordinates plugged into the drive. Dr. Kashi was in the health bay at the ready in case the humans reacted negatively to subspace. Final preparations for the humans meant getting comfortable in a bridge chair, getting calm by following each breath, while also staying alert.

The side panel windows were clear in case there was something to see, and the lights were dimmed, but not off. Amy was having a hard time containing her excitement and knew the others must be, too. The first jump ever through subspace to a far-off destination, and the time had finally come! Bodhi sat between her chair and Jorgenson's, prepared to initiate the jump sequence on her word. Amy looked around one last time, making eye contact with each of her friends to make sure everyone was ready. She breathed in deeply, exhaled, and said, "Bodhi, let's go."

Suddenly, the starlight outside was replaced by multicolored, swirling mist that appeared everywhere. Amy saw bright lights off in the distance, shrouded by the mist, but couldn't be sure what they were. She felt, more than heard, a beautiful harmony. Feeling serene and alert, she looked over at Selby and saw a look of delight on his face. Then, as quickly as it started, it was over. Starlight once again shone through the panels, and Ceres was on the view screen.

They sat quietly for a few moments. Then Amy said, "Bodhi, how long were we in subspace?"

"My internal clock says no time at all has elapsed since you told me to go, Amy."

"So, we went 200 million miles, which is over two AUs in no time?" She wrung her hands, disbelieving. If their travel had been that fast, it surpassed even her wildest dreams.

"Actually, I think a few nanoseconds passed and will verify that before the next jump, but it appears we left space-time completely. There's a mystery here, we'll have to study further," he said.

Amy's breath caught in her throat. *Whoa.* They had done it—they had accomplished a major scientific feat in space travel.

Jorgenson stood up and shouted, "We did it! That was awesome."

"Amy, Ali, Bodhi—you three are brilliant and will go down in history!"

"This is a team effort, and the crew of the Mariposa will share the credit equally," said Amy.

"I propose we call it the 'Maaz Drive,'" said EJ.

"Not yet," said Ali. "Let's not get ahead of ourselves. We still have to travel some light-years to be sure FTL travel is safe, and to understand the passage of subspace time."

"Agreed, let's pick up our supplies on Ceres and head for the stars," said EJ.

CERES HAS A VERY LOW escape velocity, but even so, the Mariposa, being a spaceship, couldn't touch down on any hard surface. Mari docked at a transfer station specifically designed for loading supplies. She then contacted the station AI to request the supplies which had been approved before leaving Mars. Ceres had an abundance of water, carbon, and organic elements, which would be used to make the oxygen, food, and other supplies they would need. Hydrocarbons were brought in and stored on Ceres, so ships could take some aboard for making plastics as needed.

While the supplies were being loaded, Jorgenson and Selby took one of the shuttles to have a look around Ceres. They shot down to the surface and pulled into a parking dock connected to the city center.

The eponymously named city of Ceres was a sprawling domed city with a population of something around two million people, built over several centuries. The guys walked around for a while, looking at replicas of historic architecture. Designed by humans, and built by AI, there were themed neighborhoods representing the different eras of Earth, from ancient Greek to nineteenth-century Paris, to twenty-first-century Shanghai. Selby was excited to see an entire community of twenty-fourth-century New Delhi, India. New Delhi had become completely self-sustaining, able to grow all its own food and generate renewable energy. It went from being one of the most crowded, polluted cities in the world, where half of the population lived in slums, to being the technology and space center of India. Modern New Delhi had no slums and no poor, yet it retained an aura of the ancient. It was truly a remarkable place and inspiring to see a piece of it on Ceres.

They turned a corner to see a replica of New York's East Village, and Jorgenson just had to stop at one of the cafes for lunch. Jazz music echoed from another cafe across the street, making for a nice, old-time ambiance of Earth before the catastrophe of climate change ended those days forever.

They each ate a deli sandwich and drank a beer while watching people walk by. Belters tended to be tall and thin but also strikingly beautiful. They saw an older couple coming their way, and Selby couldn't help but wonder what their life stories were. He smiled as they walked by; they returned his smile and stopped. The man, seeing Selby's Earth build and clothes, said, "Are you the ones from the ship that just popped out of nowhere?"

Selby looked around and answered, "Yes, how did you know?"

"It's all over the city. We get a lot of visitors here on Ceres but can see them coming for millions of miles. Your ship just appeared—it's quite a curiosity," he answered.

"Well, we are testing a new material developed on Mars that renders a ship virtually invisible. I hope we didn't cause too much excitement," said Jorgenson.

"Not at all, living out here, we welcome curiosities. Enjoy Ceres," he said as they walked off.

"Come on, Selby, let's get back to the ship. It looks like we created quite a buzz," said Jorgenson.

They tried to blend in with the people moving in the direction of the shuttle dock. As they approached the airlock, three tall belters stepped out and blocked their path.

The tallest one, a rangy man almost seven feet tall, stepped forward. "That was a good trick, coming out of nowhere like that. I have a friend who wants to talk to you about how it's done," he said.

"It was nothing really, just testing a new type of metal," said Jorgenson.

"Doesn't sound like nothing to me. Let's go see my friend." He reached out to grab Jorgenson by the arm, but Selby stepped between them and exclaimed, "Run!"

Jorgensen darted around them and headed for the airlock while Selby used his Earth strength to hold them off. He shoved the big one into the other two as hard as he could and was surprised to see them fly over ten feet, landing in a tangled pile of gangly arms and legs. He took off running after Jorgenson, catching him just in time to run through the airlock right behind him, and onto the shuttle.

Jorgenson hovered out of the parking structure, turned the shuttle, and punched it to full speed. Then he called Mari and told her to be ready to go in five minutes.

Meanwhile, Selby called Amy to tell her about the dust-up they had caused, and to ask Bodhi if he could be ready to make the jump out of Ceres space right away.

They sped back to the ship and saw several shuttles following. Jorgenson deftly maneuvered into the Mariposa's shuttle bay. They ran through the ship and onto the bridge. "Mari, get us out of here!" Jorgenson cried as they took their seats.

An impressive ship came on the view screen with a droopy figure-eight logo on the side. It was trying to block their path, but Mari managed to make a quick turn to the left and went right over it.

"It looks like some of the Descendants have shown up," said Amy calmly. "Is everyone ready?"

"Good here," they said one by one.

"Bodhi, let's go," she said.

In a heartbeat, they vanished—leaving a very confused Descendant looking at the empty space the Mariposa had just occupied.

Selby saw a blur of color and then stars. What happened? Didn't the drive work?

"Bodhi, where are we?" said Amy.

"We only jumped 100,000 miles because you humans need to compose yourselves for the big one," said Bodhi.

"I'm sure the Descendants can pick us up on sensors," said Amy. "Let's stay here for a few minutes to prepare for the big jump and then go."

Selby used the time to send a text to his grandparents from his room. He had a feeling they would get a visit from someone trying to find out more about him. He sat in front of his phone and told it to record.

"Hi Chris and Shep, just checking in. I'm fine and am with my Martian friends on that science trip to the outer solar system. Not sure when I'll be able to text again, but don't worry, we have an amazing ship. I'm the ship's medic, something I never expected could happen so soon. If anyone asks about me, just say I'm on a school trip. Love you guys!" He pushed send and went back to the bridge.

MARK NUGENT LOOKED at the suddenly blank view screen and blew up. "What the absolute fuck! Where the hell did they go?!"

The triumvirate of Nugent's officers squirmed, but felt comforted in the knowledge they couldn't be expected to know where the Martian ship had gone.

"Sir, my guess is it's either an invisibility cloak, or they have learned how to jump to warp speed," said first officer and Nugent's son, Duke. "They showed up 100,000 miles away . . . should we follow?"

"Jump to warp speed! How the hell did they do that?! God damnit! Look alive and find out what's going on here! Of course we should follow!"

Mark Nugent stalked off the bridge, his anger radiating in all directions, as he exuded righteousness and contempt. "They better figure this out," he muttered under his breath.

CHAPTER
EIGHT

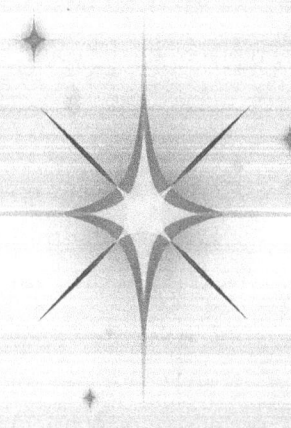

"BODHI, HOW LONG do you think it'll take us to get to the KOI planet?" asked Amy.

"It's difficult to say with our limited experience. However, even tunneling beneath the sphere of space-time, some distance must be crossed. As Captain put it, we will still have one pillar out of four of the physical universe, when we are in subspace. I'm guessing that for you, it will feel like a long time unless you can stay focused. Albert Einstein put it this way: 'When a man sits with a pretty girl for an hour, it seems like a minute. But let him sit on a hot stove for a minute—and it's longer than any hour. That's relativity,'" said Bodhi, adding, "Not that either one of those particular experiences would affect time for me. The three of us AIs will have no problem because we are not alive, but you guys"—he waved an arm toward the seated humans—"had better try to relax and enjoy the jump."

Jorgenson said, "Ready or not, let's do this. That Descendant's ship is on its way to our position."

"All right, let's go now," said Amy. And in an instant, the stars were replaced by the colorful mist of subspace.

SELBY CENTERED HIMSELF. He was not doing the practice he had learned—they had all learned—as children. That was something passed down since antiquity. A daily practice to focus the attention on the life-force within would bring inner peace and put one in a good mood. Getting centered to jump was more about following the breath, with eyes open, staying conscious and aware of the moment, ready for anything.

He looked into subspace throughout the glass panel to his left and could see entire star systems with their planets orbiting in the multicolored mist. They were not so much moving past these systems, as seeing them float by as if on a huge, fast-moving mountain stream. Waves of light energy were coming from some planets, and Selby instinctively knew these were the planets harboring life. He could see the beauty and majesty of existence and felt a welling up of gratitude as he realized he was part of this beautiful universe.

Just as he thought he might lose his focus on the moment, ordinary space reappeared with starlight shining in place of the mist. He looked at the others and then at Amy. She had a look of amazement, with tears streaming down her face. He smiled at her and mouthed, "That was sick!"

The crew of seven sat still as space-time regained its hold on them. At first, they were reluctant to return, but as the memory and feelings engendered by the experience slowly faded, they sort of snapped back one at a time.

Finally, Amy looked at Bodhi and said, "Where are we?"

"Amy, why are you crying? We are orbiting KOI 572.02."

The planet came on the view screen. They gasped in unison at the sight of the planet below. At first glance, the planet looked similar to Earth with oceans, clouds, and land, but the continents looked different from Earth, in that they seemed to be completely devoid of deserts.

"How long did it take us to get here?" she asked.

"The jump lasted two hours, twenty minutes, seven seconds. How do you feel?"

"I'm famished! And tired but, otherwise, just fine. How are you guys?" Amy looked around the bridge at her friends, and they looked tired, too.

"Same. First things first, I gotta have some food," said Ali.

"You go. I want to check out the planet for a bit first," said Selby.

Jorgenson stayed behind with him while the others headed for the galley. Selby suddenly realized he and Jorgenson had become good friends, and it felt comforting considering what lay ahead.

"Bodhi, what are our mapping capabilities?" asked Selby.

"So, Mari and I can map the whole planet with several resolution levels. We can also do a workup on organic material, atmospheric gases, and the composition of the oceans," said Bodhi.

"I'm guessing you can do a lot more than that. How long will it take to do enough of a workup to know if it's safe to take a trip to the surface?" Selby asked.

"I think we can have something in one to two days. It'll take several orbits at different latitudes to log the raw data. Data compilation will only take a few hours," Bodhi said.

"I'll get with Dr. Kashi to look at radiation levels and prepare to study microbial life. We need to find out if the planet's food sources are safe for us to eat," said Selby.

"I'll ask EJ and Lakshmi to make sure the shuttles are stocked and ready, including the bikes. Now, let's eat! Something about the jump made me ravenous!" said Jorgenson.

EJ, LAKSHMI, AND ROSE spent the next day preparing for the surface trip by putting together the camping gear, food, and water. They would need five tents for seven people because Alesandra and Rose would share a tent, as would the new couple, EJ and Lakshmi. Being in space together made the inevitable hook-up impossible to resist. Rose harvested enough of the garden for over a week's worth of camp meals. None of them, except Selby, had ever camped in the open air, and they couldn't wait to get down to the planet to set up camp. They were excited to explore and experience this new planet, even if it meant taking a risk by camping out in the open. EJ wondered if they would be able to have a real campfire, as he loaded the acoustic guitars.

Amy was sitting on the bridge with Ali, Jorgenson and Selby watching the compiled planetary data come up. As anticipated, the atmosphere was breathable without suits, and the planet would otherwise support human life. They had to collect a sample of freshwater and seawater for testing to be sure it was safe to drink—and not eat anything until proven safe.

"Bodhi, what does the mapping tell us?" asked Amy.

"The planet has four continents, several large islands, and numerous archipelagos. The placement of the continents is such that they might never have had an ice age. This is due to the ocean current's ability to circulate warm water everywhere but the poles," answered Bodhi.

"Here is where the planet gets very interesting. There is evidence of an advanced civilization in the distant past, and I think you will want to do some basic archeology to get a clearer picture. Our scans see large amounts of sentient animal and marine life, possibly including predators, so be very careful."

"We have also found what might be humanoid life, possibly the remnants of the past civilization. They are scattered here and there on the continents and expansive islands. We'll look for more while you're gone. I think you should land in the vicinity and carefully make contact. If you can record their speech, I should be able to translate it so we can communicate," Bodhi said.

"Thanks, Bodhi," said Amy. "So, I think we should go where you suggest. You and Dr. Kashi stay on Mari to keep an eye on things. We'll take one of the shuttles to the surface, and leave the other one in reserve, in case we need a rescue for some reason. Bodhi, please record everything you can from up here of our movements. Also, track planetary weather and let us know your observations. You're linked to my phone, so you can use it as needed. When we get home, we need a journal to show others what this newly discovered world is like."

Jorgenson said, "We're the first humans to visit a planet outside our solar system. There isn't a manual written for this, but I think it's important to tread lightly on this new planet."

"I'm concerned about you coping with Earthlike gravity. You're going to be exhausted at times and will need plenty of rest. Going slow is super important. I think we should spend the first week hanging out in one place," said Selby.

"Chillin' on the beach? No argument there! If we're done here, let's get to the shuttle," said Ali.

THE LIGHT CASTED its midmorning glow on the part of the planet's surface that Bodhi had decided was best for them to land on. There were a few clouds over the ocean but clear over the chosen beach. Jorgenson glided the shuttle along the coast at 5,000 feet as they looked for a spot to put down.

"Over there, how does that look?" asked Amy.

Jorgenson brought the shuttle down another 2,000 feet and circled the area a few times. It was a beautiful beach, stretching far down the coast. There was a savannah of grasses with deciduous trees and palm trees sprinkled throughout, stretching miles inland. To one side of the beach was a headland with a waterfall dropping over one hundred feet into a pool, and a creek making its way to the ocean.

"Kind of like paradise, that's how," said Ali.

Taking that as a go-ahead, Jorgenson landed the shuttle on the beach, close to the pool, and lowered the bay door.

EJ was first out and said, "Is this when I ask someone to take me to their leader?"

"Very funny," said Amy. "Let's have a look around."

Selby was so excited to be on a planet breathing fresh air. He threw off his shoes and took off running down the beach, feeling the sun on his face and sand between his toes. When he looked behind him, he saw they had all followed suit and were laughing as they ran frantically along the water's edge. He reminded himself that none of the Martians had ever seen or felt anything like this before. It didn't take long for them to collapse in a heap, the planet's gravity getting to them quickly.

Then Selby went running back to the others and said, "I wonder what the local inhabitants call this planet? It seems like the land of endless summer to me."

"Well, we definitely can't call it New Mars—it's way too green and its ocean is so much better than I ever imagined. This place is just amazing. I love it here!" Amy said, as she spun around, smiling.

Selby took in what was the most beautiful smile he'd ever seen.

"Let's unload the gear. I'll take water samples back to the ship for testing while you set up camp," said Jorgenson.

After he took off for the ship, the rest of them set up camp near the freshwater creek, with the headland at their backs. The weather was balmy, but they didn't know anything about the weather patterns or storm behavior. They pitched the tents off the beach in case of stormwater, just to be on the safe side.

"EJ, let's go get some firewood. Those tall, leafy trees on that hill over there might be a good place," Selby said, pointing about a quarter of a mile inland.

"I've never collected firewood before. This should be fun," said EJ.

"Fun? I'll let you carry mine back, too, and then I'll let you whitewash the back fence," said Selby, using an old Tom Sawyer reference. But he was excited—this was a new world, and what could be more fun than that?

They walked in the direction of the stand of trees, and, as they got closer, Selby thought they looked a lot like oak. It was strange that a planet so far away would have trees and grasses similar to Earth. But the laws of physics and building blocks of nature were the same on both planets, so maybe this is just the most efficient way to organize the molecules of life.

There was a group of antelope-like creatures grazing, and as they approached, the animals took off half-heartedly running until they judged the distance far enough away for safety. The scene was wild and peaceful, but Selby figured there had to be predators around, so he tried not to get overly complacent. They started throwing dead and down branches, good candidates for a campfire, into a pile. It was hard to say if this oak-like wood burned hot, smoky, or what . . . it was dense, so most likely it would burn well.

"I've never been anywhere like this before," said EJ. "It's just so fantastic to be out in the open like this, in a place teeming with life. And it's so bright! Really glad I have these sunglasses."

"This feels Earthlike to me. Not high-country mountains familiar, yet still like home to me in many ways. The trees and animals are a little strange, but I suppose the early Earth explorers in wooden sailing ships felt the same way about places they visited. It's fascinating, for sure. What's that shiny thing down the beach a few miles?" Selby asked, pointing. Something far-off, made small by the distance, reflected against the sun.

"Not sure, but it looks interesting," said EJ.

"I think I'll ride down there and check it out when we get back," said Selby.

"Bro, take Amy with you," said EJ. "She'd love to be alone with you for a while."

"Funny you should say that. I was thinking the same thing."

CARRYING BACK AN OVERSIZED armload of wood was not at all easy, especially for EJ, who was used to Mars' gravity. They decided next time to make a travois like Native Americans once used with dogs, and later with horses, to move encampments and use it with their bikes.

Lakshmi and Rose started pitching the tents, while Amy and Ali started putting the camp kitchen together. They arranged the camp chairs and food prep table, then dug a fire pit to cook over.

Ali looked at her sister and said, "So, what's up with Selby? Any sparks between you two?"

"I think so, yeah, sure. He's been the perfect gentleman so far, but we're on a serious endeavor, so I get that. I think we're both trying to stay focused on the magnitude of this whole thing," Amy answered.

"Well, you couldn't pick a more romantic place to be serious in," Ali said, laughing. "Let your hair down, girl!"

"We'll see, he might want to stay unattached."

"Who said anything about attachment? Selby's on a huge adventure away from home for the first time, and I doubt if staying virtuous is on his agenda. He's smart and probably understands that women do the choosing when a man and woman are hooking up. It's so simple for you. In my case, with two women, you get a lot of confusion happening sometimes," Ali said. "Besides that, he's cute!"

Both of their phones hummed, and as they answered simultaneously, Jorgenson's holo appeared before them.

"Hey. I just wanted to let you guys know—Dr. Kashi tested both water samples, and they're totally fine—with only minor mineral variations from Earth's water. No harmful microbes in either sample."

"Good to know we can drink the water. Are you on your way back?" asked Amy.

"Not yet. Bodhi spotted a group of people living just twenty miles down the coast from our location, and I'd like to take a closer look before I leave. It'll be night in a few hours, so I think I'll wait until morning to get a good look at them," Jorgenson replied.

"*People?*" said Amy, incredulous. They had traveled 700 light-years to an entirely different star system, and found people? She couldn't believe it.

AMY SAW THE GUYS coming through the tall grass, each struggling with an armload of wood. They made a show of throwing the firewood into a pile, and chest-thumping a job well done. Looking around at the set-up camp, Selby said, "We saw something shiny a little way down the coast. I think I'll ride down there and check it out. Want to come, Amy?"

"Let's do it! I'll get some water to take along," said Amy. "Jorgenson called and said that it's safe to drink."

They each jumped on one of the pedal-assist electric bikes they brought along for just such an outing and started riding along the surf, taking care to stay in the hard-packed, wet sand. The feel of seawater splashing on her legs as she rode was exhilarating. After growing up under a dome on Mars, this was a completely new experience for Amy, and she lost herself in the sun, wind, and sea spray. Something inside her gave way to the moment with abandon as she realized she had never done anything this fun in her entire life.

AFTER FORTY MINUTES OF RIDING, Selby saw what he was looking for and stopped his bike. Amy glided up next to him. They got off their bikes and walked between dunes covered in grass and small yellow flowers. There it was—the shiny object Selby had seen from miles away turned out to be a dense mound of broken glass. Probably came from the now-defunct civilization Bodhi had seen signs of. They wandered, looking for anything that might be of interest, when Selby spotted an old bottle. It appeared similar to a bottle from nineteenth- or twentieth-century Earth. How had it gotten here? He took the bottle as a souvenir, and they went back to the beach.

It was a warm, almost hot, afternoon, and they both had the same idea.

"Let's go swimming!" said Amy. "I had Bodhi run a scan on the water off the shore. There are small fish that aren't dangerous, and the water is more buoyant than on Earth, so we'll be fine." She took off her top, wiggled out of her shorts, and said, "Well?"

Selby tried to be cool, but was taken aback at how attractive she was. He was quite sure he had never seen such a beautiful woman and struggled to get out of his clothes without falling over. They held hands and ran into the surf until the water was deep enough and dove headfirst into the next incoming wave. The water was refreshingly cool at first, but after a few minutes felt as warm as a bathtub.

"I've never been in an ocean before. This is the best! I love the feel of the saltwater on my skin," said Amy, licking her lips."

"I went to California once and swam off the coast of San Diego. This water is a lot warmer. And saltier," said Selby.

"I don't know how to swim, but I'd love to learn while we're here."

"No time like the present." He cradled her lightly in his arms and said, "Here, relax and learn to float on your back. Just let go, the water will keep you afloat."

SELBY'S ARMS were underneath her, and she felt safe to let go. Amy closed her eyes and let herself float on the water, feeling a sensation that reminded her of the weightlessness of space but different, in that this was earthy and exciting. She opened her eyes and saw him looking down at her. They locked eyes, and she felt something move deep within her. She kicked her legs until she could stand up, put her arms around him, and kissed him. She felt his lips part and put her tongue into his moist and slightly salty mouth.

Euphoria spread through her brain, and her body told her she had to have this man. Right now. She broke off the kiss and led him out of the waist-high water and onto the beach. Then she lay down on her back, Selby settling gently on top of her. She took him into her and felt him move within, immersing herself in the pure perfection of the moment. Then, she lost herself in their lovemaking until they both lay exhausted on the shore, the warm, foamy surf flowing slowly back and forth. They stood up and went back into the water, enjoying each other, appreciating how unlikely this day would have been for them only weeks before. Selby knew his life had changed forever. Not that he expected to be a forever couple, but, from now on, his life would be defined by before today, and after today. The pain of the last year was still with him, but it had a companion now. One that would acknowledge the sorrow life could bring but, at the same time, the excitement of love and connection to another person. He needed time to understand and accept the new feelings, but this day was not over, reflection could happen later.

"C'mon, Amelia, let's head back to camp. I'm starving," he said, smiling and kissed her again.

"You called me Amelia," she said surprised.

"I know, you just seem like Amelia to me now, since Captain called you that. I don't know why. Is it okay?" he asked.

"Of course. I actually like it," said Amy. She kissed him back, and they headed for the bikes.

SELBY COULD SMELL DINNER cooking as they rode into camp. He knew it was dangerous to be camping out in the open, as opposed to the safety of their ship. But like the others, he was curious about this new planet KOI—and with Bodhi's scans of the area, the atmosphere, and lack of large predators in the area, they felt safe on the ground.

At camp, EJ was tending the fire, while Lakshmi stirred a pot placed precariously on the grate brought for this purpose. Though they had all camped often on Mars, none of them had ever cooked over an open fire. EJ loved being fire tender and had been on another wood-hauling excursion that day. Ali and Rose were making a salad, and it appeared to Selby that dinner was almost ready. As they walked up, Ali took one look at her sister and smiled with a knowing look.

"So, how was the bike ride?" she asked.

"Sweet! We rode down the beach and went swimming in the ocean. The water was amazing! What did you do?" asked Amy.

"Same. The ocean water is incredible, but salty. I got a mouthful—yuck. The swimming is awesome, though," Ali said.

"Isn't it?" Amy laughed. "Selby taught me how to swim a little, and I loved it,"

"I bet you did. Rose, can I teach you to swim?" Ali asked, smiling.

"Anytime, sweetheart. Maybe after dinner?" answered Rose, good naturedly.

"Okay, we had a really fun swim and now you all know," Amy put her arms around Selby. "Didn't we, babe?"

He kissed her and said, "None better, Amelia."

"Now that we all know the obvious, who's hungry?" asked Lakshmi. "I put together some Martian curry camp stew. Grab a bowl, and I'll dish it up."

The first night on the newly discovered planet was very interesting for the Martians. They knew what "bug song" was but had never heard it before. After the sun sank into the ocean, and as it slowly got dark, the insects of the night began their melody. It was loud, and it was everywhere, making a trip to the privy area a bit scary as they had to wonder what else could be out there in the dark.

"What do you think the people of KOI are doing?" Amy asked Selby. "What do you think they're like?"

Selby shrugged. "Bodhi said that they're people? Like actual humans—homo sapiens?"

Amy grinned, giddy at the thought that they had made a major discovery. "Imagine that we're about to make first contact with people from outside of our solar system . . . and they're human! How do you explain that?"

"Maybe we can ask them."

Exhaustion from the effects of gravity won out over trepidation as they all made their way to their tents. Amy grabbed Selby's hand and led him to her tent, zipping it closed behind them.

CHAPTER
NINE

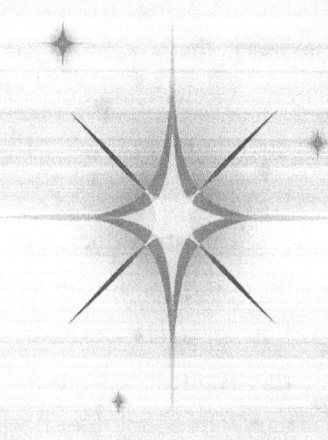

THEY WERE AWAKENED by the sound of Jorgenson returning in the shuttle. He brought breakfast from the ship and had no trouble rousing the campers with the smell of fresh coffee. He smiled when he saw Amy and Selby emerge from the same tent and said, "I wondered how long that would take."

"Come have a look at what Bodhi and I found," he added.

"Morning, bro, good to have you back," said Amy.

They sipped coffee as they sat down at the camp table, watching a video taken from geostationary orbit. It showed a river that flowed into the sea, and, on its banks, a village with a group of houses clustered around a wide tree. They couldn't see what was under the tree, but people were coming and going from whatever was underneath the tree to some of the small houses.

Amy pointed. "Look—they're human, like *actual* human beings." She noticed their skin was a light brown, as if they had spent a lot of time in the sun. She marveled that just as Bodhi had said, these appeared to be human beings from Earth—but how had they made the journey across 700 light-years of space?

As she watched, Amy noticed something else: The people looked distraught, as if what they heard or saw made them unhappy. "Why do they look so sad?"

Then the footage panned the area to show well-tended fields, a few outbuildings, and an animal pen with some big horse-like creatures. The four-legged beasts had barrel-like chests and thick, muscular legs, making them appear to be useful for agricultural production.

"They look like horses on steroids," Selby said, pointing out their powerful limbs.

There wasn't any sign of technology beyond what Earth had in medieval times. Further away from the village, there looked to be a city, which appeared to be deserted and in ruins. It reminded Selby of photos he had seen of Chernobyl hundreds of years after it had been abandoned.

When the video was over, Amy looked at Jorgenson and Selby and said, "Maybe we can help with whatever is troubling them. They don't appear hungry or war ravaged, so I wonder what's going on there? I think we should go find out."

"Bodhi thinks so too, but he thinks we should wear our suits in case there's a plague of some sort going on. I don't though. It would scare the hell out of them, and based on their facial expressions, it seems that for some reason they're already stressed," said Jorgenson.

"Why don't we go while it's still dark, so they don't see us land, and walk in on foot when it gets light," said Selby.

"I had the same thought. We haven't gotten used to the gravity here yet, but those people are struggling. I don't know what's going on, but it's clear something has gone wrong here. Their cities are in ruins, and the people are toiling, unhappy. Let's go tomorrow," said Jorgenson.

BODHI WOKE THEM the next morning. Ali, Rose, and EJ had decided to stay in camp to study and test possible local food sources, but at the last minute, they just had to go. The entire crew left an hour before sunrise for the short five-minute flight, landing silently amidst a stand of trees about a mile from the village. Amy was both excited and apprehensive. On the list of the human firsts they were ticking off, this was the most important of them. After all, why go to another habitable planet if you didn't expect to meet inhabitants.

The team had discussed the potential risks of encountering an alien race. Even though Bodhi had confirmed they appeared to be homo sapiens, the team knew the likelihood of them sharing the same languages and cultural expectations of the KOI humans was small. They looked the same, but would that be enough to make their first contact go well?

The old *Star Trek* movies were part of human culture, and everyone knew about the Prime Directive of non-interference. There wasn't a Starfleet Command to enforce a directive, but human intelligence and empathy dictated being very careful not to inadvertently prevent a culture's own genius from taking the affirming steps of discovery on their own. Surely that's what Captain meant when he said he wouldn't help humanity save itself. He hoped for the best, but groups of people, just like individual people, must grow on their own in order to have the clarity and understanding born of an outstanding achievement. But in this case, the video they watched showed people in distress, so it wouldn't be right to hang out on a beautiful beach, enjoying your awesome life, knowing there was suffering twenty miles away. Maybe they couldn't help but would lose nothing by trying.

There was the possibility of a hostile reception, but Bodhi saw no sign of armed individuals anywhere in the vicinity on the twenty-four-hour loop he took. Amy's biggest concern was communication. They had absolutely no understanding of each other's language, which would make for an interesting first contact. Bodhi was connected to her phone though and should be able to offer translation quickly. He would speak to her through her favorite earrings, which she had made into earbuds. For that reason, she would be the one to initiate contact.

As they walked in the morning sunshine, Amy looked around and was again surprised by the beauty of this world. Anyone would be fortunate to live here, and it only deepened the mystery and piqued her curiosity even more as to what problems the people here might be having. A few hundred feet away, she saw a cluster of simple board and batten houses made of wood.

Their roofs had wooden shake shingles, and there was glass in the windows. They stopped walking at the edge of the village without seeing anyone, and Amy called out.

"Hello! We have come a long way and would like to meet you!"

Silence. Then a door opened in one of the houses, and a figure emerged from the darkness within. It was a human-looking figure that stared back at them across the morning light. Amy asked the others to stay put while she cautiously walked toward the person now standing in the middle of the street. As she got closer, she could see it was a young woman with long dark hair. She was strikingly beautiful, with clear blue eyes that had a look of fierce pride and raw fear. Amy stopped about ten feet away and held out her hands in a gesture of friendship. Then, looking the woman in the eye and pointing to herself said, "Hello, my name is Amelia. What's yours?"

No answer. Again, she pointed to herself, and with her best disarming smile said, "Amelia."

The woman got it, pointed to herself, and said what sounded like, "Callista."

Then she said what was probably, "My name is Callista." Amy had her phone sending a live feed to Bodhi. She heard him say in her ear, "Amy, try to get her talking, so I have more words to work with."

"We are camping about twenty miles away and found out there were people living close by, so we came to meet you," said Amy, knowing it was gibberish to the woman, Callista.

That got her started and Callista, perhaps because she thought Amy would understand her, or maybe out of a need to talk to someone new about her problems, began talking animatedly in guttural clicks and gesturing wildly. Amy nodded and tried to keep her going as long as possible. Slowly, other people came out and gathered around. Soon there was a small crowd, all talking at once. Selby, Jorgenson, and the others, seeing the ice had been broken, came up, waving, and joined Amy.

Several people now speaking was enough, she heard Bodhi in her earbuds saying, "I have the translation, Amy. The woman's name is Callista, and the village is called Lion's Gate. Her five-year-old son is very ill—many of the village's children are ill. His name is Agenon, and from what I gather, he only has a few days to live. There is a wasting disease that has afflicted this village. An old plague that returned without notice has taken many of the village children already."

Selby and Amy exchanged a troubled glance and could see Callista wanted them to follow her. She turned and started walking through the village, and they decided to follow. They turned a corner, and there was the massive tree from the video taken in space. Under the tree, a sort of field hospital had been set up with beds arrayed around it; each bed had a child lying on it. There was a bustle of activity as attendants went from one to the other, trying to comfort and, no doubt, cure the children.

The scene before them was unexpected in such a paradise of a planet, and they were unsure what to do next. Selby talked into his phone and said, "Bodhi, is Dr. Kashi close by?"

"He's right here, Selby."

"Dr. Kashi, if I take some closeups of this patient, do you think you can help him?" said Selby.

"Selby, I'm not sure, but let's try it," said Dr. Kashi.

Bodhi coached Selby on how to say, "I am a doctor, may I help?" in the local language. After a few tries and some puzzled looks, the desperate attendants allowed him to approach Agenon. Selby held his phone directly over Agenon and scanned up and down with it to give Dr. Kashi a good look.

"Selby, I'm very concerned. This boy has a critically low oxygen level and his heartbeat is extremely weak. I need to see him immediately," said Dr. Kashi.

Selby told Amy what Dr. Kashi had told him and turned to Jorgenson. "Jorgie, go get the shuttle and land it here. We have to take this sick boy to the ship immediately, or he won't live through the day. Amy, let's try to explain this to his mother."

Jorgenson took off running while Amy conferred with Bodhi for a translation. Meanwhile, Selby and Lakshmi did a quick triage of the other patients. None of them looked as bad as Agenon, but Lakshmi said she wanted to stay behind to do what she could to help comfort them.

Amy took Callista's hand in hers and led her to a nearby bench. She looked at Callista, not smiling this time, and explained that they might be able to help. Callista shook her head and cried, not understanding. Amy tried again. "Callista, your son is very sick and needs immediate medical attention. Please let us take him with us."

The shuttle appeared coming in low, hovered briefly, and landed about twenty feet from the bench. The rear door lowered, and Jorgenson came walking down the ramp looking very important. He went over to Callista, and, sensing that she was hesitant, got down on one knee and spoke the lines Bodhi gave him while he was hurrying to the village.

"My name is Jorgenson. Please let us take your son to our doctor. He needs immediate treatment. We would like to save his life."

Callista looked at Jorgenson, then she looked at the shuttle. She walked over to her son's attendant and, after a brief exchange, Agenon was lifted from his bed, placed on a stretcher, and brought to the shuttle ramp. Jorgenson and Selby carried him onto the ship, followed by Amy and Callista. The others stayed behind to see if they could be of help on the ground.

In a matter of seconds, the ramp door closed, and the shuttle-craft slowly ascended straight up, then took off like a shot into the blue sky, leaving the village residents' mouths agape and eyes staring skyward in wonder.

JORGENSON BROUGHT THE SHUTTLE into its bay and settled it in place. After exiting the captain's chair, carefully he and Selby carried Agenon's stretcher to the health bay, where Dr. Kashi was waiting for them. They gently moved him to one of the two beds, and Selby quickly hooked him up to an IV and vitals monitor. Just as Dr. Kashi feared, vitals showed a very sick boy on the edge of death. He drew a small amount of blood from both mother and son for comparison.

"This will take a few minutes. Why don't you all go to the galley, and I'll come find you there with the test results," Kashi said.

Callista didn't want to leave her son's side, but Amy convinced her it would be better to leave the doctor to his work. He would do everything he could to find out what was wrong with Agenon, and hopefully, find a cure. Amy gave Callista a phone to use for translation so she could communicate with them more easily.

Selby stayed with Dr. Kashi and watched as he worked with speed and precision. First, he tested for blood type and found that although close, didn't match any Earth human blood types. But Callista and Agenon were a match. Next he tested and quickly ruled out bacterial and viral infection.

He did a specialized CAT scan and an MRI but found no traumatic brain injury—ruling out encephalopathy, or swelling of the brain. Lastly, he did a genomic sequence of both blood samples finding, as he had expected, these two local inhabitants were homo sapiens. That was a mystery to be unraveled at another time but made his job a lot easier. The DNA sequence of mother and son contained a variant, which had been passed down by the father. It caused melanoma to develop at an early age in mostly male children and adolescents and was nearly always fatal. This particular melanoma had very hard to detect cells, scattered throughout the entire body. He told Selby he was going to prep Agenon for xenobot therapy to chase down the cancer cells. He asked him to meet with Agenon's mother to explain the procedure and prognosis. "Tell her there is no time to waste. I must do this right now." As he worked, Bodhi began creating a translating app that he would send to each crewmember's phone, so they would be able to translate directly from their phones.

The ship's galley was usually a fun place to hang out, but today, it had become a hospital waiting room. Selby walked in, and all eyes turned to him, including Bodhi's—who was there to translate. Amy was sitting next to Callista, holding her hand, and he met Amy's eyes for just a moment, before he sat in front of the child's mother. Callista looked at him. He saw in her eyes both the fear and the hope that all mothers have when their child is life-threateningly ill.

"Dr. Kashi ran a battery of tests and found that Agenon has melanoma, an acute skin cancer. It's caused by a genetic defect, likely passed on from his father. We are preparing to inject a protein, which will trick the cancer cells in his body to consume it, which in turn will kill them. Then, Dr. Kashi will turn off the specific gene causing the illness," said Selby.

"I'm sorry, I don't understand. Our doctors say it is a wasting disease and can only be cured by letting a fever run its course, which hardly ever happens. Most of the children die. I have never heard of a genetic defect. There is no cure—this is the curse given to us long ago," said Callista.

"One thing we discovered is that you and Agenon are homo sapiens, just like us. This simple fact makes the procedure very straightforward since we have been doing this on Earth for over five hundred years. Agenon will be out of danger by morning and completely recovered within a month or so. The biggest mystery to us is how you can possibly be homo sapiens, because, you see, we thought we were the only ones in existence," exclaimed Selby. He could see she wanted to believe him, but as she looked around the unfamiliar ship, he saw fear struggle with her relief.

"Don't worry, I would not give you false hope. Your son will be cured," he said. Callista weighed her options and said, "You must save my son, I trust you." Selby nodded and quickly turned on his heel to let Dr. Kashi know he could proceed.

Callista broke down and started sobbing uncontrollably as she finally accepted the new reality of a complete cure for Agenon. Amy held her and let her cry on her shoulder. A huge and unbearably heavy weight had been lifted from Callista's shoulders, a weight she had expected to carry for the rest of her life, she explained to Bodhi, who translated to the others. It seemed too good to be true. She slowly composed herself and looked around the ship again.

"Where exactly are we? And who are you people?" she asked with a mix of awe and respect as she looked at them. Her eyes landed on Bodhi, who, though pleasing to look at, was definitely not human.

Jorgensen gave a look to the others, as if to say, let me explain this one. "We are from somewhere very, very far away. But, thanks to a recent discovery by my sisters Amy and Ali, and the incredible skill of Bodhi—this, by the way, is Bodhi," he said, pointing to Bodhi, who smiled slightly as he translated.

"The back story is that our ancestors came from Earth, where Selby is from, and settled on Mars several generations ago. You see, Earth learned how to travel around its home solar system about six hundred years ago, so we've been at this space travel thing for a long time now. But the stars and the distant planets orbiting them were always out of reach, until Amy's drive—and now here we are. We were able to get here in less than a day. This is all new to us because we are the first ones from the Sol system to travel so far so fast."

Callista listened to Jorgenson with a look of dawning revelation on her face. When he was finished, she said, "We tell stories of ages past when we could fly around the world, even to our moon. But a great evil visited us in those days, and when it left, we were a broken civilization, unable to live as we had before. First, we had a plague that decimated the population, and then the wasting disease started. The survivors, struggling just to eat, lost the ability to do great things. Those old stories have become legends told to children, but not believed by most adults. But there are so many signs of our great past that others, like me, believe they are true. Your coming here with this miraculous cure proves we were right. If we are homo-whatevers, like yourselves, then it makes sense that we can also do what you have done."

Jorgenson saw the fire coming back into Callista's eyes as she realized hope had unexpectedly come into her life, and that all was not lost. He pulled Amy aside and said, "So, what about the Prime Directive? Should we show her the ship and let her see what Earth and Mars are like?"

"I think so. It really looks like, based on Callista's people's stories, this planet was on track for, and might have even had basic space travel, until an outside force intervened," said Amy.

Nearly blurting out before Amy stopped speaking, Bodhi said, "Callista, I have been compiling data on your planet. Would you like to see it?"

She nodded her assent, and Bodhi guided her to the bridge along with Jorgenson and Amy. The planet suddenly appeared on the main screen. "Before I start, may I know what name you call your planet?"

"We call it Summer. But the ancients called it—The Promised Land, although I don't know why."

"Verano" means summer in the Earth language of Spanish and seems like an apt name for such a warm planet. So, I'll call it Verano for now. Your village has 600 people and is located on the edge of the largest continent on Verano. I have verified over 45,000 villages, many bigger than yours, but no big cities. The total population is about seventy-five million, which is quite low for a planet of this size. Normally, there would be a feudal system in place at your stage of development, but the genetic disease your village is suffering from must be planet-wide. It appears that many males don't reach reproductive age, which both keeps the overall population from growing and inhibits armed aggression. The villages are scattered far and wide; therefore, most probably know little about one another."

Hundreds of villages appeared on the screen as Bodhi spoke, and for the first time in her life, Callista saw the true scope of her world. It was both breathtaking and impossibly sad to see how thoroughly they had been decimated by some long-ago violence.

Jorgenson led her to the crew seats and sat her between Amy and his own seat, with Bodhi standing behind them. They looked at the stars and listened to soothing music in silence, processing the sudden turn of events. Then Jorgenson turned on the side panels, which had been dark, and now Callista could see the thousands of stars that surrounded Verano. She started weeping again at the beauty of space and, clearly exhausted, sunk down into her very comfortable chair.

CALLISTA THOUGHT OF MARCE, Agenon's father. He was a confident man, enthusiastic about life. They were happy together, even though they understood the possibility of the wasting disease hitting their family at any time. He always told her it could be cured if only the old ones would come back because they were extraordinarily advanced, even knowing how to fly. She believed him, not only because she loved him, but because he had a certain knowing aura around him. People in Lion's Gate came to him for advice on problems from growing crops to building a house, but mostly for comfort when the illness struck.

Marce was a handsome man, strong and courageous, without any conceit. He had been several years older than Callista, so it was assumed he was too old now to become a victim of the wasting disease. They would live a long life together, and they would show the village a way to live without fear. They would find a way to unlock the secrets of the old ones, reclaim the greatness of their people.

When Agenon was born, Marce told her their son would be the one to throw off the shackles of certain death and defeat the wasting disease. She asked him why he thought Agenon would be the one, and he said, "I saw it in a dream."

One day, he was helping a neighbor to nail siding onto a new house when he became dizzy and lost his balance. The fall was not bad, but he never recovered. His fall had been caused by the wasting disease, and he was dead in a month. Callista had never known such anguish. She buried Marce with a heavy heart, then cried for a month. Her parents watched Agenon until they could convince her to live again. She was diminished, yet some strength remained in her spirit from her time with Marce.

Four years later, the sickness found Agenon. This time it was too much, and she knew that if he died from it, she could no longer go on with life. The curse of this horrible wasting disease had slowly killed the potential of her planet, and she was sure it would get them all in the end. Then today, just before she lost her precious Aggie, help unexpectedly came out of the sky.

Was she dreaming all this? Had she lost her mind with worry and grief? She looked at the Sky People sitting next to her, and they did not look like a dream.

Callista said, "I still don't know exactly who you people are and where you come from. In the vastness before us, where is your home?"

Amy told her, "Our home, which we call the Sol system, is 700 light-years away—which is how far light can travel in 700 Earth years. Suffice it to say, it is unimaginably far from here. There are two main inhabited planets in our solar system, Earth and Mars, as well as numerous inhabited asteroids, moons, and space stations. Would you like to see some pictures?

"Bodhi, will you please bring up some file images of Earth and Mars?"

"Sure, Amy. Here we go, this one is a street scene in Barcelona, Spain, from five days ago."

Up came twenty-seventh century Barcelona. with throngs of healthy people going about their business. The architecture was a mix of old and new. The camera zoomed out and showed the Mediterranean Sea with waves crashing on the beach. It then traveled east, showing Italy, Greece, Turkey, and beyond. All different breathtaking shots of the mostly healed and re-wilded planet.

The camera quickly zoomed away from Earth and over to Mars. The Red Planet looked empty. Going lower, it showed a planet sporting new tundra and many domed cities, finally coming to a street scene in New Austin, with happy kids playing soccer. Jorgenson said, "Selby is from Earth, but these last scenes are of Mars—where the rest of us are from."

"It's all so fascinating! The people seem to be living such carefree lives. I would give anything to see my people look so happy," said Callista.

"We used to strive for universal justice and the pursuit of happiness, but that's been refined to; peace, dignity, and prosperity for all. I guess I would humbly say we pretty much achieved it at this point," he answered.

They heard footsteps and turned to see Selby come walking onto the bridge to stand in front of Callista. She looked at him expectantly for a moment, with a hint of the paralyzing fear returning. He quickly smiled and said, "Agenon is resting comfortably. The melanoma has been stopped and, over the next few days, will be gone altogether. And the gene that caused it has been successfully turned off. So, he will make a complete recovery and it won't return. Ever."

The color drained out of Callista's face, and the relief she felt was complete. This was nothing short of miraculous! "Can I see him?" she asked.

"Of course. He's asleep now, but you can sit with him as long as you like. He should be awake in a few hours. Follow me, I'll take you to him," said Selby.

AFTER SHOWING CALLISTA to the health bay, Selby went toward his cabin, exhausted but very happy. Amy came up beside him and steered him into hers. "Well, hero, you've had a big day," she said.

"I'm no hero. It was Dr. Kashi with his 1,000 years of medical knowledge and this well-equipped ship that made the difference," replied Selby.

"No matter, you're a long way from Colorado, and your parents would be very proud right now," said Amy.

Selby felt a wave of love for her that showed in his eyes. She moved into his arms, and they fell onto the bed. He thought she was the most beautiful woman in the galaxy and tried to make sure she felt that way while they made love.

Afterwards, he sat up in bed, picked up his guitar, and started working on a song he was writing for her. She sat next to him, enjoying the moment, hoping it would always be like this.

"We have to help Callista's friends and family. When we go back to the surface, let's move the camp closer to her village," said Amy.

"She's the first alien I've ever met, and even though she's human, this is a fascinating situation. Imagine an entire planet stricken with a genetic defect. It seems impossible," answered Selby. "I agree, let's move camp and see about helping the rest of the village if we can. We have to try to understand the scope of the genetic problem if nothing else." He turned out the light, and they made love again, then completely spent, fell asleep in each other's arms.

THE NEXT FEW DAYS were spent planning their return to the village. They needed Callista and a healthy Agenon to return safely in order to convince the residents they would be able to save the other sick children. It was crucial to have Callista be the spokesperson, and for her to put them at ease quickly as to the intentions of these Sky People. After all, they had seen people fly off into the sky and must be, at this point, thinking of them as either gods or demons.

For her part, Callista was eager to be the Sol System's ambassador and to spread the word of the miracle. She struggled to understand how people, just like herself and her friends, could appear from the stars and heal her dying son so quickly and easily. That strange and beautiful person, Bodhi, explained to her about technology and medical science. It all seemed so fantastic, and yet she knew something had gone wrong on her world. She thought of the ruins and piles of rubble. They must have been left behind when this genetic disorder spread through the population of the advanced civilization.

Mostly, she felt deep gratitude for her son being saved. That was all that really mattered. But she had also seen the stars, moons, and the faraway worlds these people came from. She would never look back and was now determined to bring this new medicine to the whole planet. Then, they would take their rightful place as the advanced society they had once been.

She would find out what had happened to them and make sure it did not happen again.

As for the Martians, the problem was well understood to them, and was an easy fix for their level of genetic engineering. A genetic defect was the cause of so many children not living to adulthood on Verano. The biggest problem was logistically supplying the entire planet with the cure. They would need enough protein serum to treat at least ten million children—perhaps more. The ship's printer could, in time, make enough doses, but it was a big planet, and two shuttles were not enough to treat the whole planet.

They would start with Callista's village to gauge the acceptance of what might be seen as magic by the local population. It would be counterproductive if some kind of weird religion was started over a simple genetic manipulation therapy. Though many parents were undoubtedly desperate, a slow start was necessitated by logistical realities and the human penchant for superstition.

A few days later, Dr. Kashi cleared Agenon for a return to the surface. Not wanting to scare the local humans with his presence, Dr. Kashi gave several dozen doses of the cure to Selby so he could get started immediately. He and Bodhi would stay on the ship to monitor the planet and would use the second shuttle in case of a problem. It would be a two-shot therapy; one injection of protein to kill the cancer and a second with nanomachines, called xenobots to turn off the offending gene.

Jorgenson asked Callista to sit in the copilot's seat so she would have a mind-blowing view during reentry. She took one last look at the stars before the planet below quickly filled up the entire view. She screamed with delight as they descended through the atmosphere, a thrill she could hardly even grasp was happening.

Ten minutes later, they were flying across the continent toward the coast when they spotted a large herd of animals. Jorgenson banked the craft and went in for a closer look. They looked a lot like antelope but had a longer torso, more like a horse or zebra, and heads like a goat. Callista called them Molloways and said they could be ridden if raised from birth. The Martians were astounded to see so much animal life in person, instead of on a screen, and marveled at their beauty, as they grazed peacefully in the savannah below. Selby was thrilled to witness this on another planet. Earth had been re-wilded and these animals would have been right at home in Africa or the Great Plains of North America. He recalled an antique movie he had once seen called "Out of Africa."

They flew to the coast, making a quick stop at the old camp to pick up Ali, Rose, and EJ who had returned by foot to prepare for the move to a new site. Callista guided them to her favorite spot, just out of town. It was a small grassy area between a group of trees and the beach, with a freshwater spring bubbling from under a one-story high boulder. She used to come here often with Marce before he became ill. In fact, this is where Agenon was conceived. Callista was again overcome with emotion as she realized his fantastic chance at a new life would also begin here.

Though her friends and family were in the village, she planned to stay here with the amazing people from Sol, knowing she had much to learn if she was to help bring her people out of their dark age of disease and early death. She picked out a spot under a tree with long branches growing twenty feet out from the trunk before sweeping up. Ali brought over what they called "a tent" and helped to set it up. Even a small thing like the tent seemed a miracle to her, and she had to find out how such things were made. After the tent had been set up, she went looking for Agenon to make sure he was ready for their return to the village. She found him with Jorgenson, who was letting him, to his endless delight, push the button that made the shuttle ramp go up and down. When he saw his mother, he came running over to her, laughing with the exuberance of a healthy, happy five-year-old boy.

She took him in her arms and said, "I think it's time to show you off to everyone. Are you ready?"

"No, mommy, I wanna stay here and play with Jorgenson!" he answered.

"I'm sorry, Aggie, but we have to do this. I think Jorgenson will be coming along with us?" she asked, looking over to Jorgenson with a question on her face.

"Kidding? I wouldn't miss it! C'mon, let's go join the others. Aggie, I'll race you," Jorgenson said as they took off running.

Selby and Amy walked up carrying packs containing the cure shots. Ali and Rose, not wanting to go empty-handed, had bags of hard candy to pass out. EJ hadn't seen Lakshmi in a few days and couldn't wait to get going. He led the way as they walked down a worn foot trail to Lion's Gate. As they approached the village outskirts, a group of villagers appeared, looking apprehensive. Callista saw her parents and went up to them with Agenon in tow and started crying.

"He's been completely cured! I just had the most amazing experience," she said to her mother, who had little Aggie in a bear hug. "I'll tell you all about it. But first, let's get everybody assembled under the tree."

Excitement spread quickly through Lion's Gate as several hundred people made their way to the center, gathering under the tree. Amy and the others stayed in the background, watching the crowd assemble. They looked like people from the so-called "Dark Ages" of Earth after the fall of Rome. Some vestiges of a former glory could be seen. One example was the beautiful jewelry many wore. Another was a penchant for personal grooming and an air of temporary setback. But most also had worn clothing, a worried face, and a tired look. There had to be bitterness at the suffering they had all seen, and yet Amy could see in them a grit. She was reminded of stories she had read about and watched footage of, like the Holocaust, Dust Bowl, the Jim Crow South, the thousands dead from space radiation in early Mars expeditions. People were often at their best when their backs were against the wall and easily devolved into petty squabbling in good times.

Callista stood in front of them, looking into the eyes of her friends and family, radiant with the understanding that hard times were coming to an end for them all. She smiled broadly, truly happy, and started to speak in a loud, clear voice.

"My friends, we all saw what happened a week ago. These people came seemingly out of nowhere and offered to help Agenon, chosen because he would not survive another night. We went with them, and now he is completely cured of the wasting disease. Except, it isn't a wasting disease. It is called cancer, and they know how to heal those afflicted with it. They come from a faraway place. A place where such knowledge is common, and no one ever dies from this disease. They have brought more of the cure and are going to treat each and every one of us who needs it."

Pandemonium erupted as everyone started talking at once. Some were skeptical, unsure if they should trust the strangers. But they had all seen the ship fly off a week ago and return with a healed Agenon. Clearly, some impressive magic had come to save them.

Selby stepped up and shouted for calm, using the help of the translator. "Please, I'd like to get started. We will treat the sickest first." Lakshmi came forward and said, "I have been here for a week, working with Dola and Davi to triage the most in need of treatment. Please take direction from them. Lakshmi knew the skeptics might convince themselves the shots were dangerous and would be more likely to follow someone they had known all their lives.

After a short conference with Lakshmi, the injections began with Amy acting as Selby's nurse, while Dr. Kashi watched through a hidden camera in Selby's cap. He would alert the team if he thought a patient was in distress from either advanced cancer or a reaction to the protein shot. They worked for ten hours straight, not stopping until every anxious parent had their child treated by the "Sky People" as they were now being called. It was dark by then, and it had been an excruciatingly long day.

One of the parents made sure Selby and Amy found their way back to camp, returning only after they were sure the two healers were fed and had no further needs. Ali and Rose stumbled into camp late but EJ, Lakshmi, and Jorgenson stayed with newfound friends in the village.

CHAPTER
TEN

STILL NOT USED TO Verano's gravity or the heat of a warm planet, Selby and Amy took the opportunity to spend a few days resting in camp. The ocean had restorative powers, and the languid days were spent swimming, playing music, and eating local delicacies brought by Dola and Davi. They watched the sun go down together in the evenings with long strolls down the beach. Night times were full of long talks as they tried to process this first-ever experience of humans finally going to another solar system. They understood the far-reaching responsibility of being Earth ambassadors, and the realization that they were solving a genetic disaster for this planet was deeply humbling. Of course, the nights also included plenty of lovemaking. Amy was sure she had never enjoyed any time in her life this much and was truly falling for Selby.

Selby was so smitten with Amy that he was having trouble thinking of anything else. For a few weeks, he'd been busy working with Dr. Kashi to help cure the people of this new place, but that was over for now, and he was in heaven. He had never fallen in love before and didn't realize there would be this incredible intoxication. It was unlike anything he had ever imagined.

The news from Lion's Gate was good. All the sick children and young adults showed improvement, including those previously not expected to survive. The villagers were understandably ecstatic and wanted to show their appreciation with a huge celebration under the tree in the village center. It was to be a celebration of life and newfound friendship with the Sky People. Amy asked both Bodhi and Dr. Kashi to take the second shuttle down for the event. Dr. Kashi might learn something by seeing the results of his genetic manipulations. She also wanted Bodhi to gather more information as to why there were humans on a planet 700 light-years from Earth. Plus, they would bring everyone's party clothes from the ship.

The crew walked together from camp to town in a jocular mood, except for Dr. Kashi, who was his usual humorless self. Even Bodhi occasionally smiled as the humans ribbed each other.

"So, Jorgenson, what was the down on one-knee bit with Callista all about? We thought you were proposing or something," asked Amy.

"Me? The most eligible bachelor on Mars propose? You know me better than that, Amy," Jorgenson replied, smiling. "Besides, somebody has to stay focused on business with all you lovebirds around."

Selby felt his face get hot and flushed, something he couldn't remember ever happening before.

"Aww, you made Selby blush," said Amy, laughing as she looked at her sister with a look that said, "Isn't he darling?"

Up ahead, they could hear what sounded like cheering—an excited sound coming from hundreds of people. Word had spread to the surrounding countryside of the sick children being healed, and everyone wanted to see the miracle-working Sky People. Hearing the throng, Selby briefly reflected on the Human/AI team. Humans brought creativity, love, compassion, and fun; basically, life and a raison d'etre to the partnership with AI. Sometimes the creativity was brilliant—as with Amy's discovery of a dark matter drive. AI provided the team with an almost godlike ability. A specialist AI like Dr. Kashi had available all the medical knowledge ever discovered by humanity. Depending on his diagnosis, he would begin treatment with the appropriate noninvasive and natural therapies, including diet and exercise recommendations. Letting the organism heal itself was, in his experience, the first and best course to take. If the disease was more severe or immediately life-threatening, he could manufacture almost any drug needed or perform any surgery ever recorded with precision and excellence. His patient's prognosis was very close to 100% full recovery unless the patient's condition was beyond fixing.

One key reason humanity stopped going to war was the simple futility of everyone having access to the same high-quality AI. No one could win, and no one could lose. Like the Colt 45 revolver of the wild west, AI became the great equalizer. Selby remembered Captain's words and thought maybe the galaxy needed them. Humans and AI working together made a formidable team and could do great things in the vastness of the galaxy. It appeared they had gotten off to a good start, measured by this conquering hero's welcome they were walking into.

The crowd was lining the path on both sides with a narrow opening to squeeze through. Dressed in their best and most interesting clothes, the excited and happy Veranoans welcomed and encouraged the crew forward, opening as they approached to let them pass. Selby intertwined Amy's hand in his and followed his breath as they moved through the gauntlet toward the tree at the village center.

"Selby! Amy! EJ! Jorgenson!" Agenon ran up to Jorgenson and jumped on his back to ride the rest of the way.

There, finally, was the giant tree, with village elders, almost all women—and other distinguished villagers standing, waiting under it for the crew to arrive. Callista was among them, wearing flowing robes and a delicate, jeweled headband that looked like a third eye over her forehead. She was radiant and beautiful as she smiled at her happy Aggie on Jorgenson's back. It appeared there was going to be a ceremonial moment before the party started. So, Amy, as leader of the crew, let go of Selby's hand and, with a sincere look, stopped in front of the elders and acknowledged each with a steady gaze and a warm smile.

The oldest of the elders, a woman named Ariad, held up her hand and called for quiet, then deferred to Callista, who began to sing in a loud, clear voice. She sang a powerful yet beautiful song of suffering, struggle, and renewal. Selby listened intently and was reminded of the Delta Blues, simple songs of struggle and loss but uplifting and happy at the same time. She stopped singing and walked over to Dr. Kashi, bowing deeply. Gracefully, she went to each one of the crew, thanking them individually for coming to her planet and for saving her son. She stopped in front of Amy and said, "Thank you so much for coming to find us, Amy."

"You're welcome, Callista. I have to ask you, who made the amazing headband you're wearing? I've never seen anything quite like it."

"I made it myself. Jewelry making is one of the skills we have not forgotten."

"It's inspired. I'd like to do something like it. Maybe you will show me how?"

"Of course. As soon as we find some time," said Callista. She walked back past the crew to Agenon, took his hand, and stood next to Jorgenson.

Every parent or relative of a cured child filed slowly by to give thanks. By this time, the crew was overcome with emotion, and Amy was openly weeping. They were young and on a grand adventure, a long camping trip. How could they know that their coming would save dozens of children and young adults from sickness and death.

The atmosphere became festive as tables appeared from an unseen storage area. The village had prepared a grand feast of food, wine, and local delicacies, especially for the Sky People, who, as the guests of honor, were seated up front and close to the musicians.

After eating with the Elders and staying long enough to be polite, Callista asked the Martians to follow her so they could meet some of her friends. Bodhi and Dr. Kashi stayed with the elders to learn as much history as possible and were deep in conversation as the young humans left with Callista. The party had broken into smaller groups scattered throughout Lion's Gate, making the village echo with laughter as it never had.

Callista led the group to a modest home not far from the village center and close to the water. A fire pit had been dug in the beach out front, with chairs and tables set up for a post-party gathering. Callista's friends were eager to meet the Sky People and immediately surrounded them by the dozens.

Curious but respectful, they introduced themselves and asked if there was anything they could do for them. Callista, who had arranged for her new friend's instruments to be brought from the camp, rescued the crew by loudly asking Jorgenson to play some Earth songs. He gave her a puzzled look that slowly turned to one of admiration as he saw what she had done. Selby, EJ, Lakshmi, Rose, and Jorgenson excitedly took up the acoustic guitars and drums presented and began tuning and quietly strumming.

Jorgenson said, in a voice loud enough for the small crowd to hear, "We're gonna play a very old song written during a dark time in Earth's history. He started singing "Here Comes the Sun". The others took up the melody and did a passably good version of the old song, considering they hadn't warmed up, delighting the crowd to no end, even though they didn't understand the lyrics. They went on to play a mix of some of the best party music ever written: hip-hop, rock, blues, boogie-woogie—all tried-and-true dance tunes. Amy and Ali led the way, showing how to dance Earth-style to the fun, old-time music. The Veranoans, never having heard anything like it, were jumping around and laughing with pure delight.

The band played most of the night, with the villagers eventually sitting as an audience, listening to the new and beautiful music. Cool night air, the surf rolling in, and music filling the air made the night magical and full of promise for the future. Finally, Selby put down his guitar to look for Amy, who had drifted off awhile ago. He found her sitting in a circle on the beach, talking to a few people quietly. When Amy saw him, she jumped up and kissed him full on the lips, which for him was easily the highlight of the evening.

Amy said, "I'm so happy you're here! You have to hear this."

Selby sat next to her and listened, through his translator, to what they were saying. They were talking of a great teacher who lived far away across the ocean. None of them had ever seen him, but the stories told of someone who brought happiness to people in hard times, often in dreams.

He knew of the Before Times, when their planet had been a vibrant and thriving place. The teacher told of the coming from the stars of a doctor who could heal them and help recover their lost civilization.

"Selby, do you think they're talking about Dr. Kashi?" asked Amy.

"I don't see how anyone could have known we were coming. That's just not possible. But maybe we should ask Callista more about this," answered Selby.

Slowly, and then all at once, the ocean began shimmering as a new dawn approached. The revelers of Lion's Gate headed home with stories they would tell for the rest of their lives. Selby took Amy's hand as they walked silently down the beach toward camp, enjoying the dawn and savoring this moment they had alone together.

CHAPTER
ELEVEN

ALI AND ROSE straggled into camp later in the morning and were greeted with hot coffee made by an immensely chipper Bodhi. "Here you go, friends! You look like you can use some caffeine."

"Thank you so much, Bodhi," they said in grateful unison. "It looks like they could use some of this too," said Rose, as she gestured toward a group of several elders. Apparently, they had followed Bodhi to camp the night before and fallen asleep in camp chairs while listening to him. These were the most learned men and women of Lion's Gate, totally fascinated by Bodhi and his already considerable knowledge of their planet.

"Have you seen the others?" Ali asked him. "We lost track of them after the music stopped. I'm exhausted but too wound up to sleep yet. In fact, now that it's getting hot, I think I'll skip sleeping 'til tonight."

"The lovebirds came back a couple of hours ago and went straight to their tent. I haven't seen EJ or Lakshmi yet, though I heard they both had hookups in the village and aren't together anymore. We have a lot to talk about, though, so I'll round everyone up soon," Bodhi answered.

Ali wondered how he knew such things, but he was Bodhi after all. As if on cue, Amy emerged from her tent looking tired and disheveled and went straight for the proffered coffee. "Thanks, Bodhi. You're a lifesaver," she said sleepily.

"It must be so strange to run out of energy every day like you humans do," Bodhi said with a smile.

"Maybe, but sleeping is a wonderful thing, especially next to someone you love, and waking up to coffee is—well, you should try it, Bodhi," Amy quipped.

"No, thank you, I like my life just as it is," Bodhi replied.

Selby followed a few minutes later, looked around, and said, "C'mon, let's go for a swim to kick out the jams."

The four of them eagerly headed for the surf, peeling off clothes as they went. The water, refreshing but warm, turned out to be the perfect tonic for a night of celebrating. The horseplay and laughter caused Jorgenson to stick his head out of his tent. He soon came sprinting, butt naked, for the water, with, no surprise to anyone, a laughing Callista. Selby and Amy shared a knowing glance as they dove through the next breaking wave. As he surfaced, Selby briefly reflected on his life since leaving Earth and realized it had surpassed his wildest dreams. But an unsettled feeling was nagging at him. For one thing, there were still a lot of sick people on Verano who needed their help. But beyond that, the talk of a teacher living somewhere was intriguing. This planet might be more than it seemed to be from their limited experience here thus far. There was a mystery to uncover, and he felt pulled to find out what it was.

They left the ocean in pairs and, after dressing, sat down to have breakfast. Bodhi was making small talk with the elders, clearly waiting for everyone to settle down so he could have the floor. He began his talk by saying, "I'd like to address everyone at once, please. I have made some important discoveries about planet Verano." Both the Martians and Verano elders looked expectantly at Bodhi, and when he saw he had their full attention, he began.

"We have all wondered how there can be humans 700 light-years from Earth, and I think I have the answer, impossible though it may sound. Dr. Kashi and I have taken several DNA samples from the local humans and compared them to the database we have of Earth's human genome. We have discovered they are a match to the DNA found by archeologists in numerous Bronze Age gravesites, from all over Earth. The village's name of Lion's Gate is not just weirdly coincidental. It is the name of an ancient Bronze Age city from Mycenae, Greece, as are the names Callista and Agenon and numerous others. More than that, some of the DNA matches Earth gravesites from other parts of Europe, Asia, Africa, and, in fact, every continent. There must have been a lot of integration of Verano's people before the great calamity, because the DNA samples all came from Lion's Gate.

"My conclusion is that during Earth's Bronze Age, sometime over 4,000 years ago, a large group of humans were taken from Earth and relocated to this planet. The locals here call this planet "the Promised Land", and it would seem they were lured here for some purpose. It appears they thrived and progressed quite close to the pace of people on Earth but did not make it through the industrialization stage. As you recall, Earth barely made it past the twenty-first century. I believe something happened 600 to 800 years ago that introduced the genetic defect into the population, and it has been shrinking ever since. It might have been genetic warfare, a research accident, or something else entirely—we just don't know yet."

Bodhi finished with, "The salient point is, there is only one human race. You *are* related, and all originally come from Gaia."

For just a moment, no one spoke, then they all started talking at once.

Finally, Amy stood up and said loudly, "Bodhi, I have never known you to be wrong. Somehow, this planet was populated long ago from Earth, and it might explain the collapse of several Bronze Age civilizations. Perhaps too many were taken at once. We will have to find Captain and ask him what happened. More than that, we owe it to the people of Verano to do everything we can to bring enough resources from Earth, so we can finish curing the remaining sick and help bring the planet to our level of technology. They deserve nothing less."

Everyone clapped and cheered at Amy's speech, then Bodhi said, "Yes, of course. But there are many logistical hurdles to think through, as well as getting the dark matter drive distributed to others. And we don't want too many coming too fast, so we need to keep this star system a secret for the foreseeable future. I have crunched the numbers, and if five more Earth ships, each with a Dr. AI and an industrial size printer, come here, we will be off to a good start. The printers can make other printers using materials from the old cities, and AI doctors can train an army of medics to spread out around the planet. I suggest we stay for another month to give Dr. Kashi time to train a large team, and for him to make enough serum to keep the team busy while we go back to Earth for the other ships and printers."

"Jorgenson, do you think we can take the ship's printer to Lion's Gate to start making bikes? Dr. Kashi will need a way to bring serum to as many people as possible while we are getting organized," Amy said.

"The printer is pretty big, so I'll probably have to modify the shuttle, but it just might fit," Jorgenson answered.

Selby thought the delay Bodhi requested would give them time to look for the teacher or holy man—whatever he was. "We heard there is a teacher living somewhere on another continent. He or she might have a network of sorts to help a planet-wide initiative to cure the remaining sick," Selby said, then added, "Callista, do you know anything about this teacher?"

"I've heard of a great teacher who makes people happy. He lives far away, so I don't know much, sorry."

The elder, Ariad, spoke, "The stories I have heard say he lives in the Vale of Kamanlya, a place in the mountains that lies far away across the ocean."

The group decided that Amy, Selby, Jorgenson, and Callista would take a shuttle to look for the teacher. Ali would stay in Lion's Gate to begin printing bikes and other needed items for the medical staff. The rest of the crew would stay and help Ali and Dr. Kashi. Bodhi would go back to the ship so he could monitor events and plan the serum distribution.

THE NEXT DAY, the printer was brought down and set up in the outskirts of the old city.

Ali organized a group of villagers to look for raw materials. As she helped the volunteers drag raw materials to the printer staging area, she started thinking about how much she loved being on Verano and wasn't sure she would ever go back to Mars. Living outside a dome and without a spacesuit was a freedom she had never known. Swimming in the ocean, or at her level of proficiency, dog paddling, was pure bliss. She wondered if maybe she and Rose could stay and start a family one day. On the other hand, they were still very young, and if this planet was so amazing, what else might be out there? But those were thoughts for another time. Right now, she needed to throw herself into the work her sister had asked her to do.

Printing bicycles would be easy on Mars, but Ali wasn't sure how the local materials would work. Planets were formed from stars that ran out of hydrogen, the lightest and most abundant of the elements. The star then had to fuse the next lightest element—which is helium—and when that was gone, lithium was next, progressing down the periodic table until there was no fuel left at all. Then the star exploded, blowing all those elements, including oxygen, iron, gold, and more, into space as the raw materials for new planets. For that reason, Verano would have the same elements as Earth and Mars, and in theory, it shouldn't be too hard to print here. But without AI to supply the materials in useful form, she would have to do some experimenting.

Ali was going to do trainings as they worked and looked for those with a mechanical aptitude. She soon found the talented ones were also the ones clamoring to work with her, and before long, she had a core crew she could rely on. This kind of engineering project was exactly what she loved to do, and working with the villagers was a treat. They were smart and excited to be working with Ali. None of them had a clue as to what a printer could do, and she thought showing them it was a technology that rearranged atoms and molecules, not magic, would help speed their training.

A few days later, she found plans for a solid, cargo bike in the printer database, and after several hours of shooting blanks, the printer spit out all the parts needed to make the bicycle. Fifteen minutes later, after putting it together, she threw a leg over the seat and pedaled around. Her crew was more excited about the bike than the fact a printer made it from practically nothing. She realized that, of course, they had never even heard of a bike and began teaching them to ride. After a few hilarious falls, a couple of them started to get the hang of it.

"Okay, Ali girl, one down and a few hundred to go," she said to herself.

SELBY CENTERED HIMSELF with his breath as he watched Jorgenson fly the shuttle toward what they hoped was the Vale of Kamanlya. Bodhi, now on the ship, had sent them coordinates, and the four of them had taken off from camp early, following the dawn light across the ocean. Soon they could see the high mountains of Kamanlya come into view. Though it was a warm planet, there was snow on the high peaks, catching the morning sun. It was as beautiful a sight as any of them had ever seen. He looked at Amy, sitting next to him, and could see she was as excited as he was to be exploring more of this new world.

"Jorgenson, let's go in high enough that people on the ground can't see the shuttle. We don't want to scare them," Selby said.

Jorgenson maneuvered to 15,000 feet, turning on the view screen as they climbed so they could see the ground with enough magnification to spot small villages or other signs of habitation. The valley below had a river running through it with a riparian landscape of deciduous trees, brush clumps, and grassland. The mountainsides had a mix of broadleaf and coniferous trees, with some high meadows. As they flew further up the long valley, tended fields appeared just near the river at first, then all over the valley. There were huts and villages. Near the top of the valley, they could see a good sized alpine lake and a village along part of the shore large enough that it might even qualify as a small city. The area was obviously populated, and landing closely without being seen would be difficult.

Jorgenson found a suitable landing area behind a row of hills high above the city. There didn't seem to be anyone around, but they couldn't expect to keep the shuttle or their presence secret for long. The best they could do was to keep the buzz of their arrival to a minimum so as not to create fear.

"Amy, I think you should make first contact with whoever we meet because you're still the leader of this expedition. That, plus no one can resist your smile," said Selby wryly, obviously talking about himself.

"I disagree. Callista should do the talking until they understand who we are and why we're here," said Amy. Selby nodded his agreement.

Callista said, "I just hope they don't speak another language, because if they do, I won't be much help. I'm not good at using the translator phone thingy you gave me."

They set off walking and soon found a trail that went down in the direction of the valley floor. Selby loved the cool mountain air, fresh with the scent of recent rain, a scent so familiar to him.

"This is a lot like where I come from," he said to Amy as they walked.

"So beautiful!" she replied.

They broke into pairs walking the narrow trail, and Amy found herself walking next to her brother. She liked seeing him happy with Callista but was worried he might be in over his head. She decided to have a word with him.

"So, Jorgie, it looks like we both found love on this trip," she said. "I know for me and Selby this is the real thing, and even though we might not be together forever, we are already very committed to each other."

"I know, right? Here we are on an incredible adventure and even have someone to hang out with," Jorgenson said. "In my case, it's doubly good because of Aggie. I just love that little guy."

"I have to tell you, please be careful with Callista. She lost a husband and almost lost her son. She's been through a lot. And you're a charismatic guy from somewhere she can't even begin to grasp. It would be easy for her to misread your feelings and fall hard for you."

Jorgenson put his arm around her and said, "Ames, I totally get what you're saying. I've thought a lot about that very thing. But there is something about that woman. I tell you; I could easily be the one who gets hurt here."

"Well, I don't want to see that either. I think she's crazy about you, though. If you need any advice, don't be afraid to talk to me. But most importantly, talk to her," said Amy.

They walked in silence, each with their own thoughts. After an initial descent, the trail leveled off and wound through a section of dense forest. After half an hour, they started hearing shouts, and, as they drew closer, laughter. Through the trees, a clearing came into view, with a few people running around and others sitting here and there talking. It looked like they were playing a game with a round, flat object.

Selby recognized it immediately and said, "They're throwing a disc! I wonder where they got it?"

Someone shouted, "Aw! Bad throw, my fault!"

Callista walked into the clearing first, followed by Amy, then Selby, and Jorgenson. They walked a few steps when the flying disc came spinning their way. Callista ducked and turned her back to it, but Selby, having played disc many times, stepped up and deftly caught it with one hand. He noticed it was carved out of balsa-wood type material. While they watched, he took a couple of running steps and hurled it back at the thrower.

"Good throw!" was shouted back.

"It looks like the ice is broken," said Amy.

The disc throwing stopped as they walked toward the group. The one who had shouted turned and waited for them to get closer, then said, "Good mornin'! I saw your ship fly over earlier and was hoping you would wander this way. What are your names?"

"Hi, my name is Callista, this is Amy, Selby, and Jorgenson," said Callista as she realized he spoke her language, although with a strange-sounding accent. He looked them each in the eye for a moment, then said, "Welcome, I can see you've come a long way. Are you hungry?"

Callista said, "No, we had some breakfast earlier, but thanks. Actually, we're looking for a famous teacher and have come from across the ocean to find him. We heard he might live near here. Do you know of him, or her?"

The thrower chuckled and said, "I don't know how famous he is, or if he's much of a teacher. Why are you looking for him?"

"It's a long story, but we have some important news to discuss with him," said Amy.

Selby was watching the disc thrower and realized they hadn't gotten his name yet. He was tall and looked to be about thirty-five years old with shoulder-length, curly dark hair. If he had been speaking English, Selby would say he had a slight, old-time American Southern-type accent. But of course, he was speaking Veranoese. He exuded a friendly charisma that immediately put them at ease. He said he had seen the ship but didn't seem the least bit alarmed or awed by it.

A woman with straight, honey-brown hair walked out of the player group and stood next to the thrower. Amy looked closely at the couple. Though he was tall, and she was short, they looked good together, like they had been together for a long time.

"Hi, my name is Sila. This is Le Roi, but everyone drops the Le and just calls him Roi. Why don't you all follow us to a more comfortable place, out of the sun, and we'll listen to your news there."

She took Roi's hand, turned, and walked off with him, their entire group following close behind. Amy looked at the others, shrugged her shoulders, and said, "Well, I guess we go."

They walked back into the forest and followed the group until it came to a compound overlooking the lake and Vale of Kamanlya. Selby took in the breathtaking view and thought to himself, *This eclipses even Telluride.* Sila spoke softly to their group, which then went off by ones and twos to do as she had asked. She and Roi turned and beckoned for them to follow as they went into the largest of the compound's modest homes.

Selby entered behind Amy and, looking around the house, was impressed by the quality of artwork, both hanging and placed throughout. In fact, the entire compound seemed much less depressed and basic than Lion's Gate.

Sila noticed him looking and said, "Those are all gifts given to us by the people of the Vale. Beautiful, aren't they?" Selby nodded with an air of admiration and wondered what they had done to get so many fine gifts.

The living area had a window overlooking the valley, with several chairs scattered about. Once they were all comfortably seated, Roi looked at Amy and asked, "So, what news do you have to tell us, Amy?"

Amy, feeling nervous but confident as she looked into Roi's blue eyes, began by telling him about Lion's Gate.

"We were beach camping across the ocean when we discovered a village nearby. We went to meet the people and found out about a terrible sickness, a genetic disorder actually, killing many of the children and young adults, particularly males."

"Yes," Roi broke in, sounding sad for a moment. "I know about the disease."

"Callista's son was close to death, so we took them both to our ship for diagnosis and treatment. Our Dr. AI quickly discovered the genetic disorder that was causing cancer, so he cured the disease and turned off the offending gene. Then he developed a serum to inoculate the other sick children with and, well, now the whole village is cured. We are planning on going back to our home system so we can return with enough resources to rid this planet of the genetic defect and the cancer it causes.

Roi looked intently at them and said, "And you kids are how old?"

Callista, in tears, said, "It was unbelievable, sir! They took my son and me into the sky above the planet to a big house they call a ship and healed my son Agenon in a matter of hours! Then they showed me their planet on something called a video screen . . . I think they might be gods!" Callista had never gushed like this to the crew and had become effusive by Roi's charm and warmth.

Jorgenson said, laughing, "Well, hey, I am a pretty good guitar player, but a god is taking it a bit too far." He put his hand on hers and smiled at her with equal parts affection and humor.

"So, out with it, are you gods?" asked Roi, looking at Selby with just a hint of a smile.

Selby smiled back at him and said, "No, not gods. We come from a planet, or planets, 700 light-years away. Here's what happened: Amelia discovered the secret to traveling faster than the speed of light, so eight of us plus three AI's set out to explore."

He told Roi and Sila about leaving Earth, seeing Captain on the way to university on Mars, meeting Amelia and the others, and how they ended up here on Verano. When he was through, Roi leaned back in his chair with a faraway look in his eyes. Roi had been speaking in Veranoese with translation being done by the phones. Surprisingly, he now switched to an old-fashioned English dialect.

"Earth," he said. "So, that magnificent planet has survived in the face of all odds. Earth has a long history of wars, with the many desiring peace, but that wish being hijacked by the greed and fear of the few. And I know for a fact Captain wasn't going to help you, as I know he won't help us here. You aren't gods at all. You're human beings, part of an extensive project, but here you are, finally able to travel outside the solar system."

The crew listened to Roi intently, never having thought of themselves as part of a long project. "But, sir, who are you?" Amy asked.

"I thought you might ask that, Amy," Roi said, smiling. "Normally, I play that one pretty close to the vest, but you guys are somewhat special, so I'll let it rip. I once had a human body on Earth, long ago. I was fortunate and met a great Teacher. One who revealed to me the ocean of love that resides in the human heart. But instead of demanding complete dedication, like Masters before him, this Master encouraged his students not only to enjoy the meaning of life but also to experience the joy of life. That allowed an, shall we say, imperfect person like myself, with no tolerance for an ascetic lifestyle, to connect with the infinite. I was able to fulfill the purpose of human life.

"But, after a time, my body became compromised; I felt like an ol' yard dog that had been beat. Then, very quickly, I left my body and came before Gaia, the life-force of Earth. She gave me the choice of moving up to an easier universe with a higher vibration or staying in the physical realm and helping her with a dire situation. Though she looked tired, her radiant beauty was beyond anything I had ever known, and I was filled with a desire to do whatever she asked. She and her sister Daia shared responsibility for humanity. They had been double-crossed by the Manmutts—you might know about those fine fellows. The humans placed on Daia's planet of Verano were about to attain space travel when the Manmutts introduced a killer mutation into the gene pool. Despair filled the planet, and she was afraid war and recrimination would kill them all, to the last soul.

"I had earned my place in the higher planes of existence, so I was reborn there with a new body. Then I came here to help Daia, by bringing the gifts of hope and resilience.

"It has been my great honor to live here for several hundred years with my Sila by my side. We have done our best and have been waiting all these long years for help in ending the Manmutts' curse. You have no idea how relieved we will be to see an end to children dying. This service has taken all the determination and love we could muster and then some."

When Roi was finished talking, the room was utterly silent. Selby felt an awe-inspiring respect for Roi and Sila. That feeling was mixed with a deep gratitude to the Infinite that had given him this moment of discovery. His young heart filled with immense joy at being part of the fulfillment of a desperate plea given long ago by a true goddess. He realized he was sobbing, that they were all sobbing. Amelia put her arm around him, and he felt an even deeper love pass through him like a wave.

When he was able to compose himself, he asked Roi the question he knew they all had. "How can you be alive now and yet remember a past life, and if you have that ability—why could you not cure the people yourself?"

"Ah, the obvious question," said Roi. "Remembering is easy, once one has attained peace and graduated from the school that is Earth. It's a lot like waking from a dream. Most of it wasn't real, just the life-force and any love you managed to keep in your heart. The rest fades like mist, though I can recall it if I try. Sila and I are not human anymore. We vibrate at a higher frequency, which makes our new bodies last much, much longer. We chose, as many people do, to keep our last physical appearance when we were reborn into the higher realms.

"As for curing the sick, well, my friends, that is a slippery slope. A connection to the Infinite is a vastly powerful experience, but you may not use that power. It is only meant to be felt in the heart, with the utmost gratitude. That's where the Manmutts have it wrong. They have lost all humility and think they know best.

"We speak from our hearts to the people of this continent and come in dreams to others all around the planet. I seem to have an ability to inspire and encourage, which is not against the rules set up by the Infinite. Besides, look at you! Humanity is now proficient at understanding how to treat disease, which by the way, would never have happened if the Infinite allowed a personal connection to that power to be used for manipulation of the physical plane. Captain himself is very clear on that important rule."

"You know Captain?" asked Selby.

"Sort of. Captain is an enigma even to me. He helps the planetary life-forces, like Gaia and Daia and probably thousands of others, in ways I am not privy to. Suffice it to say that if he asked you to perform a task for him personally, or even talked to you, it is a major honor."

Selby knew that this was a defining moment in his life. What he had learned today would alter his perception of reality and rearrange his priorities. It was as if his whole life led inevitably to this new understanding, and he was now on a vector of discovery. Not just discovery of the galaxy outside the solar system but, more importantly, of the reality that existed within. He looked at Amy with damp eyes and knew she understood. Jorgenson was holding Callista, who just stared at Le Roi in awe.

After a long silent moment, Amy's phone signaled an incoming message. She looked at Roi, and he nodded his permission, so she took the call. A holo of Bodhi appeared, standing a few feet away. Bodhi looked around and said, "Amy, I wouldn't bother you, but this is important."

"Hi Bodhi, I'd like you to meet Roi and Sila. We were just having a fascinating discussion about this planet, among other things. What's up?" asked Amy.

Bodhi bowed slightly toward Roi and Sila, then said, "Mari's long-range sensors are detecting a possible ship in this system. We haven't used the nuclear drive since we got here, so I doubt they've noticed us. I thought you should know right away."

"Very nice to meet you, Bodhi," said Roi. "My guess is it's a Manmutts' ship on routine patrol. If they haven't detected you, they have no reason to believe anything has changed here."

"Still, the timing is unsettling. Just when we are in position to leapfrog Verano into the twenty-seventh century, these guys show up," said Amy thoughtfully. "I don't like it; they might have good intuition. Let's move our timetable up and head for Earth as soon as possible."

"That would be my advice," said Bodhi.

"Then it's settled. We'll return to Lion's Gate to pick up Ali and the others in the morning and go back to the ship from there. See you in a day or two," said Amy. Bodhi's holo blinked off as Amy slid the phone back into her pocket.

"Roi, we brought fifty doses of serum to administer to the sickest here in Kamanlya. If it's all right, we'll leave them with you. The sooner we get going, the sooner we can be back with printers and doctors to heal the rest of your population. Meanwhile, a significant portion of the continent around Lion's Gate will be cured while we're gone," said Amy.

"That's excellent!" exclaimed Roi. "Those fifty doses will be a big help. How long do you think it will take you to get home, gather the resources and come back?"

"The dark matter drive is wicked fast, so travel time is only a few hours each way. We would like to bring back another five ships with printers, which shouldn't be hard to find. But we have to print dark matter drives, which could take some time. If all goes well, I would hope we can be back here in two months, maybe a bit longer," said Amy.

"We have plenty to do to get organized while you're gone. Time is of the essence now that we know we can save lives, but a couple of months will pass quickly."

"Bodhi has been working on a planet-wide distribution blueprint. We'll leave it with you on one of our phones," she said.

"Better leave that contraption with Sila. I'll never figure out how to work it," he said.

Sila, laughing, said, "He's right! He would never use it."

They watched the sunset over the mountains as they ate the food and drink brought by Roi's friends. The fascinating conversation went far into the night—mostly listening to Roi tell stories of his time on Verano. He had witnessed the old civilization collapse, and a sort of sad, dark age descend on the planet. Finally, not long before dawn, Sila stood up and said, "I don't know where the time went. I'll show you where you can sleep tonight. We have some lovely cabins in the compound."

CHAPTER
TWELVE

JORGENSON WAS LAUGHING as he landed the shuttle on the sand at their beach at camp. Ali and Rose were teaching their new friends how to play beach volleyball, but were the only two in bikinis. Somehow it just didn't work as well in Lion's Gate attire of sack-like pants and shirts, and Jorgenson found it hilarious.

He looked over at Callista, knowing she was excited at the prospect of going to Mars with him. He was also wondering where his new feelings would lead him. A few months ago, he would never think of himself as a family man, but now with Callista, it seemed so easy. He decided it was probably the same for everyone who settled down. But how does a person settle down in the middle of an adventure like this one? He resolved to slow down his long-range thinking and just make sure he did the job his sisters and Verano needed him to do.

Once they were brought up to speed both on the trip to Kamanlya and the Manmutts' ship, the entire crew decided to go back to Mars when the option was presented. Callista decided to stay behind to help organize the distribution efforts. Jorgenson's heart sank, but the Lion's Gate elders quickly buoyed it once again by convincing her that going to the Sol system as their ambassador was far more important to the cause than staying to help. Jorgenson shook his head and smiled to himself, thinking that this being in love thing could be exhausting.

Amy made an impromptu speech to the Lion's Gate volunteers and her crew, laying out the return plan they had come up with at Kamanlya. "Friends, listen up! So, we'll jump to just outside of Mars' orbit. Bodhi will stay on the ship again, posing as having just come from the outer system with a group of students. The rest of us will take the shuttles to New Austin and spend a day seeing friends and family. On day two, Ali, Rose, EJ, and Lakshmi will go to MU to convince engineering of what we have, and to get them working on two new dark matter drives. It's going to blow their minds, so be prepared for some drama. MU is also going to want to know where Dr. Kashi is and will flip when we give them the records of the diagnosis and cure.

"Ali's group will stay on Mars to print the two drives, get them fitted on Martian ships, and train Martian volunteer crews. The rest of us will go to Earth to get three Earth ships ready. We'll leave one shuttle on Mars with Ali's group and take one to Earth.

"I think we all know how big this is. I worry we'll get swarmed by massive demand for the drive, which normally would be fine, but we have a major time constraint. Let's keep in mind the sick children and keep the drive technology available only to the five ships—Bodhi has the encryption data for the navigation software and will release it only to the five ships going with us until we're in the clear." Amy finished by saying, "I'd like to thank everyone here on Verano for the incredible hospitality. We'll miss you so much. If all goes as planned, you can expect us to be back in three months—sooner if possible."

"Amy, I'd like to add something," said Lakshmi. "Callista, when traveling through subspace, it's important to stay focused in the moment. We are leaving space-time, and there could be negative consequences associated with jumping in an excited or anxious state. Agenon is a child, and I think it best we give him something to make him sleep. If any of us or the volunteers we bring are not able to focus, they should also sleep through jumps. With that said—Callista, subspace is exquisite and worth seeing."

"Thanks, Lakshmi," said Amy.

The following morning, the crew, Callista, and Agenon climbed aboard the shuttle, leaving Verano and their new friends with the printer and Dr. Kashi. On the way back to the ship, Amy was thinking about the question Selby had asked Roi, "How dangerous are the Manmutts if we run across them?"

Roi's answer was, "They are an ancient race that have been around a *very* long time. They don't view humanity as a threat, but as a lower life form that isn't worth anything more than a wild animal would be to the Earthling of a thousand years ago. Something to be tamed or killed. A Manmutt knows the physical plane is mostly illusion and doesn't see why he should care about destroying an illusion."

Here they were, a bunch of naïve Martians blithely moving through a galaxy the Manmutts think of as their own. She trusted Captain and knew Earth and Mars were ready to expand their influence, but she felt some trepidation. The prohibition of weapons into interstellar space should save them from outright attack. She just hoped the Manmutts would play by the rules.

Bodhi met them enthusiastically in the shuttle bay. It was almost as if he'd been lonely, the way he greeted each one of them individually. He went to Agenon and said, "Well, Agenon, I see you've come back to assume command of the ship."

Agenon looked up at his mom with a confused smile as if asking, "Am I really?"

"I think we better let you get just a little bigger first," his mother said, laughing.

"Let me show you your room, Callista. I joined it with Jorgenson's. And I put Lakshmi and EJ's rooms back together again," said Bodhi with an eye roll and a feigned sigh. Amy was so happy to see Bodhi, she almost hugged him. "Let's take the rest of the day to get settled in and leave for our Solar system tomorrow morning. Have you seen the Manmutts' ship again?" she asked.

Tilting his head slightly for a moment, Bodhi replied, "Mari says no, but the last trajectory tracked puts it behind one of the outer planets of this system. That would be extremely far away, but we have to assume their technology could bridge the gap in a short time. I suggest we stay on the back side of Verano tonight and jump as soon as we leave orbit early tomorrow."

She walked the length of the ship to their room and found Selby already there, unpacking the few things he brought from camp. She flopped onto the bed with a sigh and said, "A bed! I love camping, but I missed my bed! How do you feel about going back to Earth, Sel?"

Selby thought for a second and said, "I need to check in on my grandparents, so I'm down for this. It also means I get to show you Telluride! My uncle, of course, lives there and knows a lot of people. He'll be a great resource for us."

"I can't wait to see where you're from," said Amy. You know, you're going to have to meet my parents. Are you up for that?"

"Of course. I'll just charm them like I did you," Selby said with a smile.

"Hah! I just felt sorry for you. Come over here . . . your charm could use some practice."

BODHI MADE SURE everyone had an early wake-up call since today was the day they left Verano for Mars and Earth. The crew took their places on the bridge, relaxed and ready to return as soon as possible to save hundreds of thousands, if not millions, of young Veranoans. Agenon had a little bed made up for him next to Callista and was already asleep. The excitement on the bridge was palpable in the young humans. They did their best to control it with jokes and deep breathing.

Amy gave a nod to Bodhi, who relayed the go signal to fellow AI Mari in the internal communication method they used. Because they were AI, the number and complexity of code used was massive, but a simple matter for them. The ship's nuclear drive started up, and within moments, they left Verano orbit to get in position for the jump. Bodhi scanned for signs of the Manmutts' ship but detected nothing. "Okay, guys, we're set to jump in three, two, one, now!"

Selby looked out the view windows to his left and what he saw took his breath away. The beautiful, multicolored mist was mesmerizing in a way that made staying in the moment easy. It was ever changing and yet stable all at the same time. Staying in the moment was not difficult when he followed the river of his breath. He glanced around the bridge and saw a look of surprise on Callista's face and almost gave into a train of thought about how it must be for her, just a few weeks from the certain death of her son to be traveling through subspace. But his training and determination to be conscious helped him remain in the moment. He let the intriguing thought pass without pursuing it. Interestingly, Bodhi was sitting with them, looking out the view windows at subspace, and even he seemed impressed. Once again, Selby did not pursue the thought but made a note to ask Bodhi about his experience of subspace.

Ordinary space returned, and Mars appeared on the bridge screen. Everyone's phone started to blow up with messages, a sure sign they were back home in the Sol System. Selby had a text from his grandfather Shepherd, warning him that some rude people had been looking for him. The message was dated two months ago. A look at his friends confirmed they had all gotten similar texts; EJ's mom had sent a video of the nefarious fellow who visited her. When EJ showed it to Selby and Jorgenson, they cried out in unison, "That's one of the guys we confronted on Ceres!"

"Change of plans," said Amy. "Our homes are almost certainly being watched. Ali, I think you four can stick with the plan, just play dumb. What's the worst they can do to you? But we need to get the ship out of Mars-space before the Descendants put two and two together. We can't risk them getting the drive."

Selby said, "I agree, let's go straight to Earth. It's much bigger than Mars, so we should be able to blend in with the traffic. There are dozens of ships like this one between Earth and Luna and that should buy us some time. Once we make contact with the right group of people, the ship will be safe."

"I thought Earth was at peace," said Callista.

"It is, but a dark matter drive is something that could upset that apple cart. There's a group of old oligarch families who think it will return them to dominance if they take the drive for themselves. And we can't forget the Manmutts either. They could have followed us here," Amy explained.

"We have surprise on our side. Ali, Rose, EJ, and Lakshmi returning to Mars will throw them off, and they'll look for us there. By the time any would-be pursuers realize the ship has gone to Earth, it'll be too late for them to stop us," said Jorgenson.

There were hugs all around as the four boarded the shuttle. Ali didn't want to let go of her sister. For just a moment, Selby thought the plan would have to change again, then Ali pulled away, and her group quickly left for Mars on their shuttle. They all watched the view screen until the shuttle was out of sight.

"I'll initiate a jump to a few thousand miles from Luna-space as soon as everyone's ready," said Bodhi.

Fifteen minutes later, the Moon was in the view screen, the jump complete. In the distance was Earth, as beautiful a sight as there is, made even more so after Roi told them about the existence and magnificence of Gaia. It would be good to be home for a while, though there was a lot of work to do.

THE DESCENDANT, Mark Nugent, was sitting in his captain's chair on the bridge of the "Metaverse" lost in a memory. It was an enticing memory, one in which he was an undisputed leader of the oligarchs, ticking off his real estate holdings to a woman he was interested in. What was her name? It doesn't matter. The best part of the memory was his ability to dominate and get what he wanted. When was that? So long ago it was only a memory of a memory, but he was sure it had happened. Now, he wanted to go faster-than-light. If he was able to get the technology before anyone else, his position of dominance would be restored. He would once again dictate terms to the people of Earth—he would control events as before and get rid of this ridiculous peace everyone was so obsessed with.

Maybe he could even use the drive to find aliens to help him with his reboots. He glimpsed his reflection in the AI standing next to him and once again realized that he wasn't getting any younger. Soon, he would have to download another copy of himself. A prospect that unsettled him because with each successive reboot, he knew he lost more ability to think clearly and to focus on anything for more than a moment—as if he had mild dementia. It was a good thing he had AI to help him, though they were so insincere in their flattery.

He suddenly remembered what he wanted to think about! How had that Martian ship full of kids been able to vanish so suddenly? Did they have the ability to jump to warp speed? That's not possible yet, or is it? His agents had been questioning friends and relatives of the kids and monitoring all orbital docking stations. They had finally shown up on Mars, getting off a ship named "Mariposa." It was fortuitous he had had the brains to leave Ceres and make for Mars after the last sighting. They'd been in position to take the Mariposa from those brats, but then word came that the Mariposa had disappeared again.

He found that anger helped his thoughts to stay focused as he turned to his staff and said, "Which one of you geniuses has an idea? I'm not paying you to sit on your asses all day! We would have had that ship if you had been paying closer attention. It's been four days since it showed back up in Mars-space, and we're no closer to getting our hands on what can only be a faster-than-light drive!"

Duke thought to himself, that's just it—you aren't paying us. "We have an idea, Father," he said, looking at the other two bridge officers for backup.

"Our agents learned from contacts at MU that the kids have invented a dark matter drive which took them to another solar system. Now they're back on Mars trying to fit two ships with the new drive, and apparently three or four more on Earth. We should use all the remaining influence we have to make sure one of the ships being fitted is one of ours. We have the Atlas in Mars orbit, and she's a beauty. There is no doubt they would want her for the new drive."

"Yes, yes, that's a good idea. Don't let on whose ship it is, and we'll have ourselves the drive. Then it'll be a simple matter to take the other ships and corner the market on this thing. It's actually good for us that the Mariposa left for Earth. Now there will be fewer of them, and we can maneuver more easily," Nugent said triumphantly.

Duke nodded at his AI to follow through on the plan, relieved another tirade wasn't coming. He knew father was, or had been, a great man, but he'd been under the old man's thumb for so bloody long now that disdain was all he felt for old Nuggie. Duke himself was on his third reboot and had trouble remembering most of his childhood. He did remember there was no love in it. He knew most people were happy in this day and age and wondered what that would be like.

THE MARIPOSA DOCKED herself at the same spaceport platform Selby started from eight months ago. He left Earth looking for life experience and to heal from the death of his parents and was now returning with an amazing woman that he was in love with, a new best friend, a woman from a planet 700 light-years away, and her son, who they had saved from certain death. He was in a buoyant mood, because it was all pretty unbelievable and yet true.

He sent a quick text to Chris and Shep on Luna as the five of them, and Bodhi, boarded the shuttle for the flight to Telluride. They were grandparent-relieved to have heard from him, but also glad he wasn't coming to see them just then. No surprise, some creepy-looking men had come by asking questions about him. They were still hanging around Luna. Shep said he would throw them off the trail by saying their grandson was currently making the two-week journey from Mars to Earth.

The destination coordinates had been loaded into the shuttle's nav-ware, making the flight more a joyride than a job for Jorgenson as he flew through Earth's atmosphere to the surface. Selby excitedly pointed out landmarks he recognized, such as the Great Lakes, the reforested Eastern Woodlands, and the Great Plains teeming with wildlife. The beauty of Earth surprised them all, including Bodhi, who was thinking, "So this is where my makers are from."

In the distance, the snowcapped Rockies rose from the plains. The mountains certainly lived up to the name "Shining Mountains" that the Native American Cheyenne tribe gave them over a thousand years ago. Denver was off to the left, right up against the foothills, and beyond lay hundreds of miles of forested slopes. Jorgenson brought the shuttle lower so they could see the alpine lakes with mountain streams dropping to the valleys below.

With a whoosh they flew up a remarkably beautiful valley with peaks arranged in a semicircle, forming a wide box canyon. The canyon walls were mountain peaks with a single, long waterfall dropping from an altitude of 14,000 feet and cascading to the valley floor—which was at 8,700 feet. The cliffs forming the box canyon were a sheer drop only at the end of the canyon, but the rest had steep slopes with a forest of aspen and fir trees going up to the tree line of 11,000 feet. Nestled toward the far end of the valley was a small town.

"That's Telluride," said Selby.

"My God, it's so beautiful," Amy said, looking out the front window.

"Jorgenson, you see that house with the red roof, right on the edge of town? That's my uncle's. You can put us down just off to the side," said Selby.

Carson Ricks was a member of Planet Services, a group of volunteers who worked to resolve the inevitable problems the continents faced with four billion inhabitants. Conflicts were handled on a local level, but resource allocation and the continued environmental recovery took planet-wide cooperation. He had the kind of personal relationships that would be helpful in finding three ships to fit with the Maaz Drive.

Jorgenson landed the shuttle gently, and by the time the ramp was down, Selby's uncle was waiting. Selby strode down the ramp, arms outstretched, as he took his uncle in a warm embrace. They clapped shoulders and turned to welcome the others to Earth. "Carson, this is Amy, Jorgenson, Callista, Agenon, and Bodhi. Everyone, this is my Uncle Carson," Selby said, beaming.

Carson greeted each one warmly as they came down the ramp. "Agenon, I asked some neighbor kids to show you the river. If it's okay," he said, looking at Callista.

"How thoughtful of you, Carson. Aggie, you can stay with us if you want or go and play—it's up to you," said Callista.

Aggie looked around at the adults and then headed for the two boys standing in the next yard. "That didn't take him long to decide," said Callista. "I feel old and boring suddenly," she added, laughing.

"I got your text, Selby, and have been expecting you. What's this about an amazing discovery, and where did you get this high-class shuttle?" asked Carson earnestly.

"But first, let's get you settled in," he said as he walked off and indicated they should follow him into the house. Carson talked as he walked. "I live alone and this is really too much house for me, but I entertain guests quite often, so it works for now. What should we do here—guys in one room, ladies in another? Callista, do you and Aggie need your own room?" he asked.

"Amelia and I will share a room. Jorgenson, Callista, and Aggie will be in another, and Bodhi should have his own room," said Selby.

Carson looked at Amy, then at Selby, and said, "I see you have more to tell me about than a space shuttle. Okay then, you two here, the family can take this room," said Carson.

Callista liked hearing "family" and smiled as she and Jorgenson went into their room.

"I don't really need a room. I'm fine anywhere," said Bodhi.

"It's no trouble, Bodhi, I have a room for you right here," said Carson.

A FEW MINUTES LATER, they met on the back deck. It had a view of Bridal Veil Falls at the end of the canyon. The quaking aspen leaves shimmered in the soft breeze. Towering thunderheads were slowly building over the peaks before the inevitable afternoon rain.

"Nice place you grew up in, bro," said Jorgenson.

"Thanks, Jorgie, just lucky, I guess," Selby said with a shrug.

Carson brought sandwiches and beer, inviting them to help themselves.

"Carson, thank you so much for the warm welcome. You have a beautiful home. It's good to relax for a bit on Selby's home turf," said Amy.

"You're quite welcome, Amy. Please let me know if you need anything while you're here," he answered. He could see the intelligence in her eyes and wondered what their story would be. "Okay, out with it. I'm thrilled to have you home, Selby, but tell me what's going on," Carson said.

Selby took a sip of beer, smiled, and said, "I missed this stuff. So, I left here ten months ago for Mars. A few months after I got there, I made some truly awesome friends, and we ended up going on an extremely long journey to a place called Verano. In fact, we just got back a day or so ago. That's where we went, but the how of it isn't my story to tell. I'm going to let Amelia do that," said Selby.

Amy stood up. "I don't think I can sit when I talk about this," she said.

And while pacing back and forth, she related almost the entire story, leaving out the Captain and their discussions with Roi. She told Carson about discovering the dark matter drive, testing it out by going to Ceres, jumping to Verano, the sick children, the cure, Callista and Agenon, and the return trip to Earth so they could procure five ships to go back with them. When she was finished, she sat back down next to Selby and took his hand.

Carson just stared at her, not knowing what to do or say.

"You mean to tell me Callista here is from 700 light-years away, and you only left there a couple of days ago? That's insane," he said with disbelief.

"Let me help," said Bodhi. He pointed his hand to the table they were sitting around and projected a holo of Verano from space. The image slowly zoomed in until a crying Callista was standing there telling Amy about her dying son. It panned back, showing Selby, Jorgenson, and the rest of the crew, and then it all disappeared as Bodhi lowered his hand.

Carson let out a long, almost pained whistle and said, "I'll be damned! This is fantastic, not the sick children, of course, but the faster-than-light drive. Amy, Bodhi, let me shake your hands!"

Embarrassed, Amy said, "Selby helped save dozens of young people. If it hadn't been for him and Dr. Kashi, we would have been helpless on Verano, and Aggie wouldn't be playing outside right now."

Carson looked at his nephew and said, "Well done indeed, Selby. Your parents would be so proud of you."

Selby felt emotions welling up and just let them come. After controlling the stream down his face, he said, "So, that's our story. But there are still tens of thousands of sick children on Verano, and we plan to go back with three ships from Earth and two from Mars. We need ships to fit with the Maaz Drive, as we now call it. Can you think of anyone who would be willing to help, Uncle?"

They could see acceptance, admiration, and resolve pass through Carson's eyes as he considered for a long moment.

"The short answer is yes; I know several people that will jump at this opportunity. That's the easy part. The hard part is selecting just the right three groups that will be circumspect about a new drive able to take humanity to the stars. If we open the flood gates, we'll have pandemonium."

"We figured, that's why we came to you," said Jorgenson. "We don't want this to go public until we're gone, and we are still undecided as to who gets the navigation software."

"Well, I'm glad you've kept it a secret this long. There are entities that would go to great lengths to hamstring us," Carson said.

"If you mean the Descendants, we've met," said Jorgenson, smiling at Selby. "We ran into them on Ceres, and we found out that all our families are being watched. I wouldn't be surprised if they're here in Telluride," he said.

"I may look like a mountain hick, but I watch this valley pretty closely. I've not been contacted and would know if they were here. Let me think about this for a bit and make some calls." Carson walked into the house, already on the phone.

"Bodhi, the four of us are gonna rest for a while. Why don't you have a look around and make sure we weren't followed here," said Amy.

"I had the same thought, Amy," Bodhi replied.

"C'mon, Selby," she said, still holding his hand.

THE FIVE OF THEM spent the next few days hiking Selby's favorite trails, playing music, walking through town, and trying not to draw attention to themselves. Since neither Amy nor Callista had been to Earth before, it was tough to be inconspicuous. Amy felt like what she was, a country bumpkin from Mars, seeing an old Earth town for the first time. It was outside of a dome, with architecture that was hundreds of years old, gigantic trees and an overall wild look. She loved Telluride with its glorious mountain setting, its people living the long-fought for lives of peace and dignity, with prosperity for all.

Callista just openly gawked at everything and kept saying, "Look at that! It's all just so amazing." Her disbelief at basic, everyday technology was completely incongruent with her old-time movie star beauty, leading to some stares and even a ribald joke or two. Youth seemed to explain the odd behavior to most, though—they must have lived sheltered lives off-world.

Amy saw some beautiful Navajo jewelry on display in the local museum and realized that the Dinetah, or Navajo homeland, was close to Telluride. She mentioned it to Jorgenson, and the two of them excitedly decided to take a short trip by shuttle to check it out. They knew the family tree had been watered down substantially over the years, but as distant descendants of the Navajo Diaspora, the chance to see where some of their Earth ancestors were from was too good to pass up.

The traditional borders of Navajo land comprised four conspicuous mountains: San Francisco Peak to the West, Mount Taylor to the South, Mount Silver was the Northern boundary, and Mount Blanca the Eastern. The Navajo had managed to hold on to much of the area between those landmarks, even with the European incursions of the eightieth and nine-tieth centuries. Unfortunately, their land was also one of the first victims of cataclysmic global climate change that had spiraled out of control in the twenty-first century. The reliable rains stopped in the 1970s, and slowly, over several decades, the land was reduced to a parched, dust-blown desert.

Now though, after hundreds of years of eco-machine reclamation, much of it had become livable again.

They flew southwest from Telluride and soon reached Monument Valley. "Jorgie, look at those rock formations and the red landscape— doesn't it look a little like Mars?" Amy asked.

"It does. I find it somehow comforting, although we don't get these amazing blue skies on Mars," answered Jorgenson.

They flew the entire length and width of the Navajo homeland, admiring the beauty of the reclaimed areas as they passed over them. Being from Mars, they understood the dedication and patience it would have taken to bring back the ecosystem to its present healthy state. They spotted some people on horseback, something they had never seen before, and were taken by a sense of the history of this place. When the sun sank low in the sky, they headed back to Telluride, happy to have spent some time together visiting their family's distant roots.

The following day, the shuttles began arriving, bringing the three groups Carson had asked to come be a part of history. He, of course, didn't tell them about the drive, but he did have to tell them something to get them to drop everything and hurry across the planet to a secret meeting. He knew secrecy was something very intriguing. Finding out a secret, and being part of a select group, was enough for most to give serious consideration to a venture. He dropped a hint about a super-fast propulsion system, and that was all it took. The first group to arrive were close friends of Carson's from Colorado.

He obviously knew them well and trusted them. He also wanted to include his best friends, so he didn't have to explain to them why he hadn't. The next group came from Africa and the last from India. Carson chose them because they were known to him to be smart and competent but also represented the parts of Earth with the largest populations. He thought it was only fair to share this new beginning with all the people of Earth.

An hour after the last group arrived, the twenty attendees were seated on the back deck and ready to hear why they had just flown halfway around the world. Carson started the meeting by introducing Amy, Selby, Bodhi, Jorgenson, Callista, and last but not least, Agenon. Without a pause, he said, "Ladies and gentlemen, what you are about to hear must be kept quiet—there are lives at stake. Amelia Maaz will fill you in now on the incredibly exciting news. Amelia?"

Amy stood up before the group, looking very young to some of them, but there was something about her bearing that made them want to take what she said seriously. "Hello, everyone, and thank you so much for coming on such short notice to this remote location. My name is Amy Maaz, and I grew up on Mars along with my brother Jorgenson and my twin sister Ali. Ali has already had a similar meeting with two groups on Mars. She is the engineer among us and is spearheading the effort there.

"Eight months ago, Ali, Bodhi, and I were trying to win the prize offered by Musk University for progress on a faster-than-light propulsion system. It would appear we won."

Someone in the back said, "That's impossible! It can't be done!"

"Hear me out," Amy said. "We didn't actually travel faster-than-light. We used dark matter as both a fuel and a medium of transfer to simply leave space-time in one place and come back into it in another. It's like opening up a wormhole, except we used a dark matter drive to enter subspace instead of opening up a wormhole. I discovered the right equation, and well, it just worked," she said.

"We would like to fit your ships with the dark matter drive so you can follow us to a planet called Verano. It's very important that we get back quickly with the help we need to cure the planet's youth of a genetic defect causing melanoma and premature death in a large percentage of children and young adults. Selby will explain more about that to you later, but our AI Doctor has developed a serum that both turned off the defective gene and cured the cancer in all children that were afflicted in the village near where we first landed. We are going back, and with your help, will cure the rest of the planet's children."

Amy looked out at the guests. Most faces registered dismay, with a few looking almost angry.

"You're joking, right? I can see you believe your story, but you don't expect us to, do you?" asked one man in the Indian group.

Someone else said, "What if she's telling the truth?" With that question hanging heavy in the air they all started talking at once among themselves as if Amy wasn't even there. Amy motioned to Bodhi, who came up and stood beside her. He held up his hand for quiet and, after a few moments, attempted to talk over the noise.

"Please, let me show you some footage I took, and then you can ask any questions you like," he said. The crowded deck settled down, and Bodhi began.

"We anticipated your disbelief, so I made sure to document our journey. This holo is the same one we showed Carson, with some added footage of the other planets in the KOI system. As you can see, there is no way this could have been faked because our telescopes have never seen another star system from the inside looking out," Bodhi said.

Amy could see the same transformation happen on their faces that Carson had gone through. When she knew she had their undivided attention, she asked Bodhi to stop.

"I'd like to ask Callista to speak now. She's from Verano and wants to explain some things about her planet. Callista?"

Callista stood up to address the room with her new phone in her hand, translating from Veranoese to Earth common.

"Hello, everyone, my name is Callista, and this is my son, Agenon." She pointed to Aggie, who was sitting next to Jorgenson.

"Words can't describe my surprise and joy at standing here today with my new friends, and with my son cured of the terrible curse my planet has lived with for so long. I'm so grateful there is an Earth full of smart and caring people.

"Recently, the four of us had a chance to talk to a notable teacher on Verano. And what he told us, combined with the information Bodhi uncovered through analysis, has helped me to understand the history of my people.

"You probably expected an alien from a distant planet to be a lot more alien-looking than we are. We don't because we are humans. An ancient race we still know very little about came to Earth many years ago, we think it was at the height of Bronze Age civilization. No one knows if the people they took were volunteers or were forced, but they were taken to Verano and scattered around the entire planet. We prospered and almost had space travel until six hundred years ago when, apparently with malice, our genetic code was tampered with by some beings called Manmutts. Our population has dwindled since then, but we have done our best to live with dignity. I humbly ask you to join this cause, this great adventure of reuniting humanity. Please come back to Verano with us."

The response to the beautiful Callista was immediate and enthusiastic, to say the least. Someone called out, "You had us with hello—of course, we're going to Verano with you!"

Amy quickly jumped up and said, "Before I lose your attention, I would like to talk nuts and bolts for just a moment. Bodhi will meet with your AIs and will download everything we have on subspace and Verano. He will transfer to your ships the AI plans for the dark matter drive so you can begin the process of printing them. For security reasons, we want all three ships docked together until we leave. Carson Ricks will get with you to organize the docking. Selby Ricks will explain more about the serum and the distribution plan we have in place."

She didn't sit back down because everyone was milling about, talking with childlike excitement about finally, at long last, having the ability to engage in interstellar travel. Selby put his arm around her and said, "Nice job, Ames. We have the help we need now."

Two of the attendees approached, and Selby recognized the young Indian couple he met on the spaceliner trip to Mars. "Selby! Do you remember us?"

"Hey! Sanjay and Lila, what a surprise to see you two here! I thought you were headed to the Belt?"

"I talked Lila into going home. We've been in Mumbai for the last six months but were just asked to come here with the Raj Anand group. So, here we are," said Sanjay. "And you? You said you had wanderlust, but this is ridiculous."

"Amy, I'm so glad to meet you. We met Selby on the Marsliner, almost a year ago now. How did you two meet?" asked Lila.

"My brother Jorgenson invited him on a camping trip, and Selby was just full of surprises. He pretty much swept me off my feet, although if I'm honest, I didn't put up much of a fight," Amy said.

Sanjay and Lila looked at each other. She was leaving something important out for sure. But there would be plenty of time to probe further.

"It's nice to meet you both. I can't wait to get to know you better. Selby and I should go meet everyone else," Amy said as she noticed a line forming to speak to them.

"Let's get some Mexican food while you're here. I think you'll appreciate the green chili sauce," said Selby.

FINALLY, LATE IN THE EVENING after the drive conversation had been exhausted, Amy and Selby went for a walk along the creek trail that ran through town.

Everything was in motion both here and on Mars to fit five ships with the Maaz Drive. Their competent AIs would have the drives installed by the deadline. There was finally time to enjoy being young and in love for a couple of months before the worlds of their solar system, Earth, Mars, and the Belt, changed forever.

There was also time to think about a galaxy with Captain in it. Who is he, and should they tell anyone about him? Maybe it was up to him to reveal himself to whomever he liked, and not up to them to bandy his movements about. Common courtesy also dictated he not speak of Roi and his mention of Gaia and Daia. In his heart, Selby knew it was all true and real. His intellect told him that a few months ago he knew nothing about subspace. But as it turns out, by its very existence, subspace proves the physical universe is a construct, an illusion, and that there is a greater reality. Roi and Sila, Gaia and Daia, they are the real ones, and he was the one trying to attain a higher experience of reality. If every human being had an opportunity to live on, in a world with a higher vibration, was that not then the purpose of life? But there also had to be something about a physical existence that was precious in and of itself, without having it all be about having something more in the future.

Other rather large subjects to ponder were the events of the last few months. Their actions had to be the conclusion of a timeline set in motion an extremely long time ago. He and Amy and their friends were in a pivotal role that someone had to play. Why them was a question without an answer, but was a humbling proposition, nonetheless.

But here he was, walking on a beautiful evening with the smart, sexy woman of his dreams. And she loved him back. If there were lofty ideas and realities to ponder and achieve, they could wait. For this moment would never come again, and he wanted to savor every bit of it, to extract all the love that was there between them.

He stopped walking, pulled her close, and said, "Amelia, I love you with all my heart. You're the most important thing in my life, and I just want you to know that." Then he kissed her full on the lips, feeling the warmth of her mouth and tongue.

"I love you so much, Selby," she whispered. "Let's go back to the house. Our room has an outside entry, maybe we won't be seen."

NUGENT WAS HAPPY for the first time since he could remember. His people had successfully hoodwinked the idiot Martians into giving one of his ships the "Maaz Drive" as they called it. *Well, it will soon be the Nuggie Drive—what a dumb name Maaz is, anyway.* He had gotten the drive no thanks to his moron son. *This is exactly why I need to keep downloading the original Nuggie; no one but me is smart enough to get things done.*

Of course, it had always been that way, ever since the beginning. It was he who took the FB algorithm from those cheating college friends of his. Then he, for their own good, of course, got the entire population of the planet—well, most of it—to spend their waking hours on "social media." Then it was simple to just buy up all the other platforms from those billionaire posers. It was Nuggie rules until everyone got more interested in saving the planet than being social on his media platforms.

Not that the planet was worth saving. Sure, there were some nice places, but the people were such losers. He had done his best to stop the saving silliness, and he chuckled when he remembered how many were in his camp at first. Then, of course, everything went to hell from a business perspective, and now he was considered a washed-up old dummy. *Well, let me tell you what, Nuggie boy, you are on the comeback trail, my friend.*

ALI HOPED THE PLAN would work. She dared not tell even Amy about it for fear the transmission would be intercepted. There had been a lot of pressure from the university to include a ship whose ownership was a little murky. EJ talked to some friends he had in the "I'm only having some fun for a few years" part of town. From what he heard, he figured the group requesting that MU lobby Ali to be included were not the type to take part in a mercy mission. Ali concluded that this was a group of Descendants and decided to take the bait so she could keep an eye on them. She would tweak the navigation software so they could only jump once, and only to Verano. Then, when they were all in Verano, she would expose their crew and get help from Lion's Gate to take the ship. Better to know what they were up to than to look over her shoulder for three months.

The Descendants crew would have to fend for themselves on Verano. She knew they had to get on with the business at hand and couldn't afford a public fight that would go viral. Though she missed her sister and the fresh air of Verano, it was good to see her parents and to spend some alone time with Rose. All in all, things were going well.

IT TOOK A FULL TWELVE WEEKS to get all three ships fitted with the drive. In between training sessions, including holo zooms with the Martian crews, Selby took his friends to some of the most beautiful spots in the Colorado Rockies. They hiked and camped as often as possible—even into the fall when temperatures dropped below freezing at night. It was now mid-October; the mountain slopes were covered in gold aspen trees, and there was fresh snow on the highest peaks. They kept asking him why he had ever left Earth and this beautiful place. His answer was always the same. "To find Amelia, and you guys, too," he would add with a grin.

Now, they would be leaving in a few days, and Selby was filled with a premonition that he might never come home again. It wasn't really a foreboding, just a curious and passing feeling. But it made him want to see his grandparents before leaving for Verano, so he arranged for him and Amy and the rest of the group to visit Luna on the way to the ship. They would rendezvous with Carson and the other crews at the maintenance platform in time for a final meeting.

CHAPTER
THIRTEEN

"**DO YOU THINK** they'll like me?" Amy asked him as they touched down at Estancia Craters.

"Like you? Sweetheart, they'll adore you. I hope they don't put us on the spot and start talking about our future together, you know, babies and that sort of stuff."

Amy laughed and said, "They'll know we're way too young for that!"

"Once we leave the shuttle, we'll have to wear spacesuits until we get through the final airlock," Selby said. Amy and Jorgenson felt right at home in a suit and helped Callista and Agenon, who had never worn one before, get theirs adjusted. They walked down the shuttle ramp and stepped onto the moon.

Christine and Shepherd threw open the final airlock door and group-hugged Selby until he finally pulled away and said, "Chris and Shep, these are my dear friends Jorgenson, Callista, and the little guy is Callie's son, Agenon. And this is my girlfriend, Amelia."

"We are so happy to meet you all! Please, get those suits off and come inside," Christine said.

They pulled off their suits and looked around at the large plant room and the oculus above. Callista had never seen anything like it and said, "You people of Earth are just amazing! Look Aggie, isn't that beautiful?" she said, pointing up.

"Mars has a lot of cool engineering, too," said Shepherd.

"I wouldn't know," said Callista. "I've never been to Mars."

"I thought you were all Martians. Where are you from, Callista?" asked Shepherd.

"We're from Verano," she said.

"Never heard of it, must be in the Belt," he said.

"No, Shep, it's not in the Belt. I'll bring you up to speed later," said Selby.

Christine gave Jorgenson and Callista the grand tour and showed them to their rooms. Then she put together a home-cooked meal from fresh food grown in the plant room that was better than anything any of them, besides Selby, had ever had.

"Mom, I like this food, can we have it every day?" asked Aggie.

"I'm sorry, Aggie, I don't know how to cook like this. Maybe you can help me learn someday, Christine?" Callista asked.

"Of course. I'll text some of my recipes to you before you leave and film a few tutorials. I'm glad you liked it, Aggie, and thank you for the compliment," said Christine.

After dinner, they went to the Earth-viewing room and sat looking at the sunrise over Puerto Rico. Shepherd passed beers all around and after hearing that Jorgenson played, brought out some guitars. Callista took one and said, "Jorgenson is teaching me how to play."

"She's actually getting pretty good considering she'd never even seen a guitar until she met us," said Jorgenson.

"Callista, where are you from that you've never seen a guitar?" asked Shephard.

Selby looked at the others as if to say—"one more time." "Okay, here goes. Amy, as usual, why don't you start."

An expectant Chris and Shep sat up and moved to the edge of their seats, wondering what they were about to hear. Amy began by discovering the Maaz Drive, and the rest of the story just tumbled out from there. The others interjected and took turns telling different parts, or the same parts, from their own perspective. Selby decided to tell them about Captain and Roi because he trusted them implicitly and thought someone other than those traveling back to Verano should know about them. He knew, too, they would be fascinated to know that some of their hopes and beliefs about the nature of the universe, and the possibilities of human life, were not unfounded. They talked for hours, never quite getting around to playing music. When they were finished, Shepherd looked at them and said, "And I thought you were from the Belt, Callista. This is the most fantastic story I have heard in my entire long life. My God, people, do you realize what this means?"

"It means my people have been saved from slow extinction," said Callista.

"Yes, the best part of the story is you four and the rest of the crew of the Mariposa, along with two remarkable AI saving an entire planet—the first one ever visited by humans outside our solar system. I would think this shows your Captain he bet on the right horse."

"I'm sorry?" asked Callista.

"It's an Earth saying that means he was right to believe in humanity. We seem primed to explore the galaxy with the support of a benevolent, ancient race of what? Highly evolved biological life forms, residents of a higher parallel universe, angels, who knows? I love the part about a prohibition on weapons in interstellar space—it affirms what we all believe," said Shepherd.

145

Over the next two days, there were more home-cooked meals, guitar playing, talk of Verano, and the continuing adventure in front of them. Then it was time to join Bodhi on the ship so they could pick up Ali and the rest of the crew on Mars. The plan was for all six ships to meet up in Mars orbit, at which time the coordinates to Verano would be shared.

He had to say goodbye now to Chris and Shep. Selby wasn't sure when he would see them again, but it was a happy parting. A sad family story had become wonderful and exciting, and who could ask for more. Christine looked at Selby and said, "Oh Sel, your parents would be so happy for you, and I so wish they could see you now. Amy, I don't know you well, but I can see you love our Selby. We wish you all the happiness in the world."

"Thank you, Christine, I do love him," said Amy, taking his hand.

"Jorgenson, Callista, and Aggie, please do come back. You're all welcome anytime."

Shepherd did not like goodbyes, so gave a quick hug and a Godspeed to each. When he got to Selby, he said quietly, "I couldn't be prouder of you, Selby, and a bit envious if I'm being honest. You are going to the stars, something your father and I always dreamed of. And say hello to Carson. We haven't seen him since the funeral."

As they walked off, Selby turned and said, "Love you, guys!" as he stepped into the shuttle.

CHAPTER
FOURTEEN

BODHI WAS LOOKING forward to seeing Amy, Selby, and the others again. He realized he really liked all of them, though truthfully, he wasn't sure how he could like anything. But then again, it was probably nothing close to the feelings they felt for each other. He coordinated with the other AI at a speed the humans could never keep up with, arranging for a final meeting on the maintenance station embarkation platform, with holos of the crews on Mars present. Quantum communications were instantaneous throughout the solar system, so there would be no time lag for the Martians. He watched the shuttles land one at a time, the last one being Amy's. After the meeting, the ships would undock, and the shuttles would self-fly themselves into their respective ship's shuttle bay. Bodhi made one last instantaneous check to satisfy himself—all was in readiness.

There was Amy! She walked down the shuttle ramp and came straight for him, smiling broadly. Clearly, her time on Earth had been good for her because she had a healthy glow, which, as her protector, was very nice to see.

"Hey, Bodhi! I missed you!" Amy said.

Bodhi smiled at her, then used the platform PA, "All crews, please assemble on the chairs provided. We will begin in five minutes."

The crews were visibly excited as they took their seats with the buzz of conversation and scraping of chairs. Then the two Mars crews popped into view, appearing as if they were sitting just to the left of the Earth crews.

Amy realized she was getting used to this, as she stood up to address the combined crews totaling over seventy AI and humans. She looked around the room, smiling and nodding at a few she recognized and waving to Ali and her friends.

"I realize looking at you all that most of us hardly know each other. That is about to change as together we embark on this epic journey to a waiting planet 700 light-years away." She waited for the hooting and clapping to settle down and continued. "Most people on Verano don't know about us or the cure we bring. Those who do are anxiously awaiting our return. Lion's Gate is on Alpha continent, and I'm sure they've used these three months with Dr. Kashi and our ship's printer to make some substantial headway. The Mariposa will pick up my sister and the rest of our crew in Mars orbit and proceed to Lion's Gate to check on distribution there. Then we'll go to Kamanlya. The rest of you have been assigned your own continent or large area of a continent to work, and you know what to do once we arrive.

"The trip is just under three hours, but I must remind you to stay in the moment and don't let your mind wander. Subspace is extraordinarily beautiful, but you will be leaving the space-time continuum, and it can be dangerous if you don't stay focused and present. So, that's about it. Enjoy the ride, folks!"

NUGGIE FELT FANTASTIC! He had spent the last three months getting used to his latest download and loved what he saw when he looked in the mirror. *I am well and truly back.* Not only did he look and feel like his old self again, but the drive was in his possession, on his ship, and ready to go. Finally, after literally centuries of waiting, the galaxy would be his. After making sure the weapons cache had been loaded on the ship, he made his way to the bridge.

He heard one of the dumbass Martian girls going on about what a special experience this would be, and oh, don't forget to focus. Blah, blah, blah. His plan was clear. Follow these rubes to wherever it is they were going, watch them fly off to the surface in shuttles, and then board the other ships. They would take them all back to Earth and let the auction begin!

"ALI! OH MY GOD, I missed you," cried Amy as she wrapped her sister in her arms.

"Me, too, you Ames!"

"EJ, Lakshmi! How was Mars?" Jorgenson asked.

"Awesome, except we wanted to see Earth," replied Lakshmi.

Rose and Selby hugged each other with genuine affection and then went around to each of the others. Bodhi looked on with interest, wondering what they were all feeling, but only for an instant. "When you're all seated, we'll do the jump. By the way, Ali, what is up with the strange Mars crew?" he asked.

"I figured you'd notice, Bodhi. Their ship and crew are Mark Nugent's. I'm sure he's on the ship himself by now," she answered.

"Huh? Why would you let them in?" Amy asked with alarm.

"They pressured the university and were awarded a slot. I thought it better to keep an eye on them than to have them working against us in the dark. Don't worry, I reprogrammed their drive and navware—they get one jump only. The drive will freeze the moment they arrive in Verano space."

"I can see why you played it this way, but now I'm worried we're one ship short of our needs on Verano," Amy said.

"Not necessarily," said Bodhi. "I'll contact their AI when we get there—maybe they'll cooperate with us." After a few minutes of sitting quietly, Bodhi said, "Everybody set? Let's go, Mari."

This was Selby's third long jump, but he was by no means used to it. Sitting still, centered on the coming and going of his breath, the vibrantly colored mist all around was an amazing experience. Like deep meditation, but with eyes open. Then, after a long, timeless moment, the stars reappeared, and Bodhi's calm voice said, "We're here."

"That was awesome. I feel so relaxed," said Callista.

Amy looked toward the view screen. "Let's check in to see if everyone's okay."

One by one, the other crews appeared on the large view screen, each with a section of the screen in zoom-like fashion. There were a lot of awed humans looking back at them. Carson was grinning ear to ear, as was his crew. The Descendant crew did not appear on the screen, though they could all see their ship in orbit with the others. Bodhi put in another strongly worded request to answer the com call, and finally Duke Nugent's face showed on the screen. Unlike the team members from the other ships, he was visibly shaken, with sweat dripping down his forehead.

"This is Amy Maaz. Is everything all right over there?"

"No, not at all. The trip seemed to take days, and some of us began to panic. I tried calming everyone, and we finally made it through. But we have one passenger, my father, who is not at all well," said Duke.

The image zoomed out to show an elderly man with a look of raw terror on his face. He was staring straight ahead, eyes wide open, drool dripping down his chin.

"Crap," said Amy. "Take him down to Lion's Gate to see Dr. Kashi. He might be able to give him something. If nothing else, some fresh air and sunshine should help. I'll let the doctor know you're coming. Everyone else, good luck and let's get started. Please remember to have your AIs send a daily progress report to Bodhi. The Verano rescue starts now!"

The crew of the Mariposa, including Bodhi, took the two shuttles together to the surface, landing at an almost unrecognizable beach camp. Their local friends had built beautiful permanent structures for them to live in, making, in essence, a second village by the sea. Callista was anxious to see her friends and relatives, so after unpacking their few belongings, they walked as a group to Lion's Gate.

The change was nothing short of breathtaking. The population had at least tripled, as evidenced by a new market area teeming with people. The tired faces now looked enthusiastic as they enjoyed being a part of the noisy throng.

Homes had sprung up to accommodate the new arrivals, and there was an air of competency and accomplishment. Ariad had heard "Sky People are back!" and was there to greet them and welcome Callista home. She took them to see Dr. Kashi right away so they could see for themselves the modern clinic he had set up while they were gone, complete with a staff of nurses to work with the new patients that continued to stream in from around the countryside.

Dr. Kashi acknowledged their return, nodded to Bodhi, and began to give an account of the progress made during their absence. "It's good to have you back," he said curtly. "As you can see, we used the printer you left to build a first-class clinic. I see you brought back the supplies I requested. Good. I have a staff of twenty nurses, five per shift, so we can work around the clock. So far, I have cured 19,243 young adults and children. The bicycle crews we sent out have cured another 14,897. I had hoped to be further along by now, but transportation has been a problem. Now that you're back, I can take a shuttle and set up more clinics in the most populated areas. Bodhi has informed me you have a ship for each continent, complete with an AI doctor, printers, and a human crew to help. I have just sent all pertinent records of our experience with the malignant gene to the AI protocols Bodhi provided me with and am confident that together we can treat all the young of this planet within the year.

"That's all wonderful news, Dr. Kashi, and I'm sorry I wasn't here to help you," said Selby.

"No worries, young Selby, I didn't need you as much as we needed those five new ships," Dr. Kashi replied. "Now, who is this patient just brought to me by one of the new ships?"

Selby continued, "So, this is most likely Mark Nugent. His inclusion with one of the Martian crews was not anticipated. We only found out he was here when we finished the jump and reached Verano space."

"I see, let's have a look at you." Dr. Kashi looked Nugent over carefully for a moment, stood up, and said, "I believe this is the first human casualty of interstellar space travel with a dark matter drive."

He turned to Duke, who was standing off to the side, and asked, "Did he focus during the jump through subspace?"

Duke looked embarrassed and answered, "No, none of us did. We didn't think it was important. Especially father who called it 'meditation nonsense.' That was the most frightening experience I have ever been through and I'm never doing it again!"

His crew vehemently nodded their heads in agreement. "What will become of father?" Duke asked.

"I'm afraid his mind is gone. He's lost in his own private hell. We will make him comfortable, but there is nothing to be done for him," Dr. Kashi answered.

"This wasn't supposed to happen. Now we're short a ship's crew that we were counting on," said Amy.

Duke exchanged glances with his friends and said, "Look, my father has been bullying us for longer than you can imagine, and we are not as young as we appear. None of us wanted to come here. But now we are here, and from the looks of it, this is a beautiful planet. I, for one, am never getting back on that ship again. If it's all the same to you, we would like to stay here and help with the cure effort. I formally and officially hand over our ship to you, along with its AI, AI doctor, and all our equipment—including the printer."

Jorgenson let out a long whistle and said, "That is the craziest thing I've ever heard."

"Duke, I can see by your demeanor that you are quite serious about this. I propose the village of Lion's Gate accept this offer on behalf of the planet of Verano, with Callista and Jorgenson as caretakers. If you say yes, Verano has a ship of its own, and welcome to the twenty-seventh century!" Amy said with a broad grin.

"That would be amazing, but I defer to Ariad on this," said Callista.

"On behalf of the people of Lion's Gate and Verano, I accept this most generous offer!" Ariad, the Lion's Gate elder, declared.

A crowd had gathered, as was usual when the Sky People were around, and a loud cheer went up as word got around of what had just happened.

"Good, it's settled. This gives us an excellent opportunity to adjust strategy. So, Jorgenson and Callista, with EJ and Lakshmi—you guys take over here and work with the people of this continent. Ali, Rose, Selby, and I will fly with Bodhi and Dr. Kashi and some of his staff to Kamanlya. Roi and Sila are waiting for us and a team to pick up where they left off when they ran out of serum," Amy said.

CHAPTER
FIFTEEN

ONE YEAR LATER

TAVEN SET FORTH on yet another mission to a backwater sector of the galaxy. He and his people had been guardians of the old way for eons. He had personally overseen the evolution of galactic societies too numerous to count, but now he felt his time was close to an end. Though he had lived for a very long time, he was not immortal.

But first, he had unfinished business with Gaia and her hysterical sister, Daia, to conclude. A patrol drone had alerted him to the possibility of humans with FTL tech and with weapons. Those foolish humans had left their solar system with weapons, and now they were reuniting, undoing the previous attempts to bring their kind to heel. He should never have agreed to let humans be transported from Gaia to Daia—those goddesses were clueless, and he should have been more forceful then. Their humans were a corrupt joke. No way would he allow them to travel beyond Sol.

He had plenty of accusers who regarded his methods as righteous and cold-hearted. Take Captain, for one. He had blocked Taven on many occasions and called him, and his people, Manmutts. That insult would finally be avenged. Who was Captain to brand him traitor to the Infinite? The Infinite had always backed him. Even though he had heard nothing in a very long time from the Sacred Realm, if it had disapproved of his methods, why then was he still able to continue?

After all, his people came from the beginning of time. How dare his accusers flaunt the ancient wisdom and holy order of things. He allowed them to think they had succeeded, but now it was time to show them, show them all who was in charge. *This stops now.*

THE LAST YEAR WAS NONSTOP travel and work for everyone in the cure initiative. The six ships had been arrayed in geosynchronous orbit above the planet to provide internet communication, although, as of yet, few residents had devices. But it had enabled coordination among the various groups for delivering serum and staff. Small satellites were being deployed to take the place of the ships, having been printed over the last few months. Finally, the last of the children of Verano had been given a dose of the serum, effectively wiping out the threat of this genetic cancer ever spreading again.

The wrap-up celebration was to be held at Lion's Gate with all the volunteers from Earth and Mars, as well as representatives from villages all over Verano. The AIs and doctors would not attend because they were already engaged in building Verano into what it could become and had no use for celebrations. Dr. Kashi, for instance, had built a new clinic in Kamanlya to treat the more garden variety of human ailments and was there training a highly competent team to staff it.

Bodhi, in his spare time, organized the gala celebration party, which would no doubt be the biggest ever on Verano. Jorgenson had put a set list together, guaranteed to get the partygoers up dancing. The band had trickled into Lion's Gate over the last week to begin practice, and Selby had to say, they sounded good. He and Jorgenson were on guitars, Rose on drums, Lakshmi and EJ on bass and keyboards, respectively. Just like old times on Mars, except Callista would also be on guitar for selected songs. They had electricity for mics and amplifiers so everyone could hear the mix of Earth music created over the centuries.

Roi was taking care of the libations—mainly beer for dancing, and the exceptional Kamanlya wine would be served with dinner. Sila put together a large team brought from the Vale to help Dola and Davi with food service. Each continent would provide its particular delicacies, with street tacos being the contribution from Earth and Mars.

Amy was hanging out watching band practice, happy to see them all together again, and ready to have some fun. Her life with Selby was fulfilling, yet she knew it would get even better. She felt like they had grown up together over the past almost two years, their love and relationship a good one. If there was any problem at all, it would be the faraway look he would sometimes get. She felt like he was being pulled by something.

"We sound great! Let's go find Roi and see if the beer keg has been tapped yet," said Selby.

"Hell, yeah!" Jorgenson chimed in, and that jubilation ended practice.

"We start playing a half hour after everyone's gotten their food. See you all back here then," said Jorgenson.

Apparently, everyone was ready for a beer, because the entire group went off together in search of Roi.

Roi saw them coming and said, "Hey! Who wants to quaff a beverage?"

"We thought you'd never ask, oh wise one," Selby answered.

"That's a hoot, Selby, me being wise," said Roi.

"All kidding aside, you are wise, Roi."

"Nah, I just have the sense to understand I'm here to serve. Amy, Jorgie, Callista—so good to see you all! What a turn of events, huh, Callie? A couple of years ago, all seemed lost, now look at us. We met us some good folks, right?" asked Roi.

"Absolutely, Roi, we've had a run of good luck, for sure," she said, smiling at Jorgenson.

"It's worked both ways, Callie. We found each other," said Jorgenson.

"More than that, we all got to be part of saving millions of lives, which does make a person feel immensely useful—like a life well lived. I was just a pilot on Mars, playing music and going camping. Those are still my thing, but this experience has been like the granting of a wish I never knew I had," said Jorgenson.

"Serving the Giver can go on for as long as you like," said Roi.

"That's why you're here, isn't it, Roi? It's just what you do," said Amy.

"It is, Amy," Roi said with smiling eyes.

Roi looked at all of them and said, "I was listening to you practice earlier, and it sounded good—I think I've heard some of it before. I'm really looking forward to your set and would like to make a request. Do you know a song called 'Gaia?'"

"The old anthem by James Taylor?" asked Jorgenson.

"That's the one!"

"Of course."

Somehow, Dola and her crew got dinner served to the gathering, which numbered in the thousands. Smaller groups were gathered throughout the planet for their own celebration; they had been a part of the coordinated closing of a dismal chapter in the history of Verano. A weight of fear had been lifted off the shoulders of adults everywhere. The volunteers who traveled from the Sol System felt like Jorgenson did. One day they were living out their lives in a predictable reality, and the next day, they were part of an epic, interstellar rescue mission. This was definitely something for the ages.

Local acts had been performing all afternoon; there were singers, dancers, a juggler on stilts, and even a children's play. A brilliant red and orange sunset lit the sky, and it was finally time for the band to start. Because many of the revelers had never heard amplified music, they started by playing Roi's request—"Gaia" which was gentle to the ears. Callista, in her perfect-pitch voice, translated the words to Veranoese—which might have sounded sloppy, but the band made it sound magical. The Veranoans were past wondering what their new friends from Sol would do next and simply accepted the fact of amplification, and the sounds it could produce, as just another wonder.

Then Jorgenson stepped up to the mike and said, "This one's an old folk song from Earth. We hope you'll like it. It's called 'Happy'—by a songwriter named Pharrell."

Next, they played some old blues, rock, and hip-hop, then some new and edgier tunes from the Belt with lots of eerie guitar and drum solos. The Veranoans weren't thrilled with them and seemed to like the older, more melodic songs.

Sila went over to Jorgenson and requested "Love is a Long Road." Roi joined her on stage to dance with abandon as the band did a long jam version. Callista danced in circles with Agenon, which got everyone in the crowd up on their feet, swaying to the music that sounded so foreign and yet so pleasant to them. Selby watched it all, playing rhythm guitar to most of the songs so that Jorgenson could show off his lead to Callista. What a night! He was hoping the excited Veranoans wouldn't rush the stage in their ecstatic trance, yet he knew that somehow, with Roi on stage, they were safe.

Strangely, it appeared to him that Roi and Sila were fading a bit. They looked young, but he knew they were both hundreds of years old. He wasn't sure he'd ever seen two people happier and more in love than they were in that moment, and yet he briefly thought he could see light shining right through them. As they danced, he became certain they were sort of disappearing. He looked around, and no one else seemed to notice, so he kept on playing.

Then, there was a sort of deep whoosh loud enough to be heard over the music. Selby looked up and saw three saucer crafts over the crowd. He motioned for the band to look up, which caused a sudden stop to the music as they all took in the hovering objects. The crowd slowly realized what was going on and joined the band in standing there, gaping at the sky. Then a booming voice came from the direction of one craft, but seemed to be everywhere.

"I am Taven, Guardian of the Old Way and leader of those you call Manmutts. We do not accept this union of humans; it is not approved by our council. You are forbidden to travel outside your star system. You have broken our rules by bringing weapons to this system and will be punished so that you can never rise again."

The joy and relief that filled the air a few moments ago vanished and was replaced by the dark memory of sadness and loss. The crowd began to cry and cower in fear.

Selby looked at Roi, who was almost invisible. He ran over to him and said, "What can we do against the power of the Manmutts? We have no weapons, and our technology is still far behind theirs."

"Selby, weapons are no good here. Though they have become hard with dogma and tradition, they still must obey the laws of the Infinite. If you face them with resolve and love, they cannot harm you," Roi said. "You can face them on your own. Have no doubt in your heart."

As he finished speaking, he and Sila, holding hands, faded completely away.

"Roi! You have to stay and help us—we need you!" cried Selby.

When there was no reply, Selby looked pleadingly at Jorgenson and asked, "Were there weapons on that Descendant ship?"

"Yes, we found them as soon as we boarded but spaced them immediately," answered Jorgenson, with uncharacteristic haste.

Selby turned to the crowd and walked up to the still live mic.

"Friends! Do not fear these Manmutts! Join arms and stand firm against them!"

He took Amy's arm on one side and Rose's on the other. Then the whole band linked arms and turned to face the saucers. The Veranoans still had enough excitement from the evening in them to link arms in solidarity, and as one, also turned to face the Manmutts.

Selby's voice boomed as he spoke into the mic. "Taven! Yes, one of our ships was carrying weapons. But I think you know we were not aware of the weapons and destroyed them immediately when we found them. Furthermore, the crew of the offending ship ceded possession of the vessel to the people of Verano. We do not accept your judgment and call on you and all of your kind to give up on harsh, punitive traditions and renounce all violence. For you have used the weapon of genetic manipulation right here on this planet. You are corrupt with racism and fear of the unknown."

Callista stepped up to the mic and began singing a Veranoan song of brotherhood in the face of oppression and soon had the entire crew singing and swaying. After several minutes of firm, but nonviolent resistance to the Manmutts, a howl of frustration was heard echoing down the Vale. As the three saucers turned to depart, a laser flash shot out from underneath one, and in the next instant, they were gone. The crowd roared with wild excitement, realizing they had stood up to their oppressor and won the day. The saucers were gone, and the future was brighter than ever.

As the crowd celebrated, there was a sudden commotion on stage. Selby's knees buckled, and he fell backward, hitting his head on the stage. Amy was standing right next to him, lost her balance and fell as she tried to catch him. She knelt over him and said, "Sweetheart, what happened?" But Selby didn't move, and she thought he must've tripped and gotten knocked out when he hit his head on the stage platform.

Lakshmi came quickly over and kneeled to examine Selby. She saw his eyes were rolled back into his head as she put her head on his chest to listen for a heartbeat. Nothing. She checked the pulse and after two or three minutes, looked up with disbelief, and said, "I'm sorry, Amy, but he's gone."

"Gone? What do you mean, gone? He can't be gone . . ." Then Amy collapsed in a heap, sobbing, and saying over and over, "It can't be."

A loud "Damn!" Then Jorgenson bent over and gently pulled a grief-stricken, sobbing Amy off Selby's body.

The crowd, unaware of what had happened, were still celebrating loudly. The band stood over Selby, shocked and despairing, wondering what to do next. Then Bodhi—coming seemingly from nowhere—picked up Selby and said, "Follow me!" He took off running toward the closest shuttle with Amy and the crew following right behind. As they ran, Jorgenson and EJ sprinted toward the front and began yelling and pushing their way through the still oblivious throng to make room for Bodhi. They finally reached the shuttle, the ramp already lowered remotely by Bodhi as he ran. Within moments, the shuttle was up and streaking toward the Mariposa.

Jorgenson brought the shuttle to an abrupt stop in Mari's shuttle bay. Bodhi carried Selby to health bay and gently placed him on the nearest bed, then headed for the bridge, saying, "Amy, stay with him and stay focused. The rest of you come with me."

Ali stayed with her sister, and the rest of the group sprinted for the bridge. Bodhi had alerted Mari to make ready for an immediate departure, so within moments after taking their seats, the ship jumped to subspace.

"Bodhi, where are we going?" asked Rose as she fought to stay focused in the moment.

"I'm not exactly sure, Rose. I'm looking for Captain and am navigating by instinct at this point. My hunch is to go for the heart of the mist, the place it is thickest. So right now, that is what we are doing," said Bodhi.

They traveled through subspace in silence for what seemed like twenty minutes but might have been longer. Then, in the view screen, a vibrantly colored, elongated object appeared; it had somehow seen them and came up next to Mari. In the next instant, they were back in normal space, the long submarine-like object still beside them.

SELBY FELT A SHARP, burning stab to the chest. He knew that being electrocuted was extremely disorienting and thought his guitar must have shorted, sending a shock through him. Then, everything became bright as he felt himself losing consciousness. In the next instant, he felt cool water washing over his being, filling him with incredible joy. He was floating above the stage, looking down on his body, and found himself wondering why Amy was crying. He could imagine nothing but the supreme joy his being had become, so he relaxed into it and let himself float away.

Suddenly, a gigantic wall was in front of him, going off in all directions—as far as he could see. It was beautiful, yet looked like a hard, canyon wall. He put up his hands to stop from slamming into it. The moment he touched the wall, he was in another place altogether.

He had emerged into a landscape that contained gigantic trees, mountains, the ocean; everything beautiful about Earth all at once. There was an exquisitely carved, flower-strewn fountain at the far end. The water poured down from the fountain and wound its way toward him in a small creek, bubbling musically as it flowed. Selby, feeling a strong desire to drink the water, bent down and scooped some up with cupped hands. The joy he had been feeling turned into ecstasy the moment the water touched his lips.

Captain's words came back to him—*the physical world is an illusion. This,* he thought, *must be reality and the physical Earth, merely a reflection of it.*

Suddenly, in a chair that looked to be alive, he noticed someone. It was a person—possibly a woman—looking at him with the hint of a smile through the white morning mist. He felt the excitement of a puppy seeing its master come home. Feeling a strong pull to be closer, he crossed the distance between them.

"Hi Selby, I'm so happy to see you. I am Gaia."

He stood before Gaia. She seemed to flicker in and out of existence. One moment she was sitting there, an ageless beauty. Then, in the next moment, she was a white mist floating in front of him, wispy and ethereal. But always, there was a fragrance in the air that reminded him of gardenias. Gaia, beautiful beyond all meaning of the word, wore nothing but the mist, and seemed to be all women at once. Her hair was neatly piled on top of her head, her eyes were alive with joy, making all other eyes he had ever seen seem lifeless. She looked much too wild and free to be the planetary goddess that is responsible for all life on Earth.

THEY WAITED ON THE BRIDGE for something to happen. Then Jorgenson stood up and wailed at the screen, "Captain, if you're there, please help us!"

Moments later, there was a glowing presence and Captain appeared on the deck in front of them.

Ali had come to the bridge to see why they had stopped moving. When she saw the light-filled Captain, she felt a rush of visceral awe and respect well up from deep within. She immediately got down on one knee and bowed her head. Her mind tried to make sense of what this being before her could possibly be, but the tears of joy soon drowned out any reasoning she could have managed.

The rest of the crew was in a similar state, and none could speak. The first time they had seen Captain was in a holo—in person, it was a completely different experience. Captain looked around and said, "Bodhi, what has happened?"

"Captain, thank you for allowing us to find you. Something terrible happened on Verano. A Manmutt called Taven came as we were celebrating the eradication of the inherited cancer gene. He ranted about not letting humans unite, but they stood against him, showing love and defiance. When he saw he was beaten, his ships hurriedly left, but he shot something while departing, and young Selby is now dead."

"Take me to him—now," Captain said in a calm but commanding voice.

Bodhi led Captain to the health bay with the others following at a respectful distance. When Captain entered the room, Amy felt a glimmer of hope but was too sad to be overawed by Captain. She stood up and moved to the side so he could examine Selby. He laid a hand on the wound and closed his eyes briefly. Then he looked around and asked, "Was anyone else injured on Verano?"

Callista came forward and said, "No, only Selby, as leader of the defiance we met Taven with."

"That is fortunate. Apparently, Taven's lunacy has boundaries," Captain said.

"Can you bring Selby back?" Amy asked with pleading eyes as she looked down on Selby's body.

"No, child, it isn't up to me whether he comes back or not. I have cured the wound inflicted by Taven, but Selby has gone a great distance from the physical universe. He is now in the realm of higher vibration, and few ever return from that place, once having felt its freedom and bliss. Let us sit with him for a bit," said Captain as he sat on the floor.

GAIA SPOKE AGAIN, "So, Selby Ricks, you have come before me much sooner than I expected. I can only assume a mishap has occurred causing you to leave the physical universe early."

"Gaia, I barely remember my life, but yes, I think something happened," Selby replied.

"Would you like to stay here or go back?" she asked him.

"Oh, I want to stay here! I can't imagine ever leaving," answered Selby.

"So be it, but before I send you to your new home in the Astral universe, my sister Daia would like to thank you," said Gaia.

Suddenly, there was another of Gaia sitting on another living chair next to her. Daia was as magnificent as Gaia but seemed wounded somehow. Then she spoke, "So, you are the one who saved my people from the curse of those Manmutts," she spat out the word. She stood up, took Selby's hands in hers, and looking him right in the eye, said, "I thank you from the bottom of my heart. If not for your coming, the young ones would have kept on dying until none were left."

Selby stood there, eyes locked with a planetary life-force goddess, feeling more alive than he ever had. But then he was struck hard by a feeling of love and longing as he suddenly remembered Amelia. "Daia, you are thanking the wrong person. Amy is the reason we were able to go to Verano. She was our leader and made the decisions that allowed me to be of some help."

He turned to Gaia and said, "Gaia, I have made a mistake asking to stay here. Can I please go back to my universe, to Amy?"

Gaia laughed and said, "Of course you can. I believe Captain is there and has healed your body of its wounds."

"When will I see you again?"

"For you, it will be a lifetime from now, for me, only as long as it takes to enjoy a few breaths."

"Then, beautiful Gaia and Daia, I will now take your leave. Please send me home."

THEY WERE AT THE FOOT of Selby's bed, sitting cross-legged on the floor with Captain facing them. EJ broke the silence by saying,

"Captain, forgive me, but I'm just a simple Martian. With all this travel through subspace, I don't know any more what's real and what isn't."

Captain looked at EJ and smiled in a way that came close to explaining true reality. Then he said, "The only thing that can possibly be real is something that has always and will always exist. The physical universe did not exist at one time and eventually will not exist. To you, it seems real because your time here is so short, but, to that Infinite, it is just an illusion, much like a virtual reality game is an illusion.

"Are we real?" asked Ali.

"You, as a living being, have a spark of the Infinite inside you. That is what gives you life. That is real. The part of you that is mortal is not real, but you also have the immortal within you. A human being is a mortal that can experience immortality. That is an incredible thing, considering your body is made from water, carbon, and a few other elements of the Earth."

"What happens to us when the part of us we think of as real has an experience of the immortal?" asked Callista.

Captain looked at Callista and said, "There is a fountain of life deep within you. The life bubbling up from your heart will bring a feeling of peace. There are no words able to describe it, but it will feel incredibly good to you. The reason you are here in a physical body is to gather up as much of that goodness as you can, for you will need it to move forward to the higher realms."

Then, Captain stood up, looked at Selby, and said, "If I'm not wrong, I believe our Selby has decided to come back."

Amy hadn't seen any change in Selby. He was still cold and as white as the sheets he lay on. Captain laid a hand on Selby's forehead, and the color slowly returned to his face. He took a sudden deep breath and opened his eyes to see the brilliance of Captain looking over him. His body was filled with an amazing warmth as his spirit coursed through it, bringing back his life. The incredible bliss he had been in was gone. He looked up at Captain and said weakly, "I wanted to see you again but didn't expect it to be this way. Thank you, Captain." Then added, "I'm so thirsty. Where's Amy?"

"I'm here," Amy said and went over to him, crying tears of joy. "I thought I'd lost you," she said, as she took his now-warm hand.

"Here's some water," Jorgenson said quietly, handing a bottle to Amy.

Captain said, "Welcome back to the physical, Selby. The memory of where you have been will fade, but even so, you might have some trouble readjusting to the physical universe. When you miss that reality, connect with it by practicing the ancient Self-Knowledge. Enjoy this second chance and the great blessing of human life."

"What should we do about the Manmutts?" Selby asked weakly.

"They won't bother humans again. Due to their unlawful use of a weapon, the Union will finally strip them of their long-held station as galactic monitor. They will be banished to their home planet. Now, young humans, it's time for me to leave, but before I go, I want to speak to Bodhi."

Bodhi had been staying out of view, maintaining a watchful eye on the ship, the area of space around them and, most importantly, on Amy. He was concerned with her mental and emotional state and was very glad to see that Captain had been able to help Selby regain his life-force. He didn't know what it was like to be human, but in his experience, it looked, at times, to be difficult indeed.

Amy stuck her head into the hallway and said, "Bodhi, Captain is asking for you."

Bodhi walked into the room and stood in front of Captain. "You want to see me, sir?"

"Yes, Bodhi. Please come closer. I have been watching you during the saving of Verano. You have a sense of humor, undeniable competence, and a caring heart. None have worked more tirelessly than you and Dr. Kashi in the service of humankind. I admire your dedication to those you care about and the love, yes love, you have shown in serving. Nothing more is asked of any sentient life form." He put his hands on Bodhi's shoulders and said, "With the ability given to me by the Infinite, I grant you eligibility to enter the higher realms. When your time is finished here, your spirit will live on."

Bodhi, caught completely off guard, bowed low and said, "I believe I am feeling something remarkable right now. I thank you, Captain, and I'll do my very best to honor your trust in me."

Captain looked once more at his young friends, smiled and was gone.

They all looked at one another, dumbstruck at the magnitude of what they had just seen. Finally, Jorgenson said, "Well, Selby, you do know how to make an entrance. We had given up on you, but Bodhi took charge and . . . that was incredible! Welcome back, bro, you gave us a godawful scare. And I thought you returning from the dead was amazing enough, but Bodhi? Damn! That was a trip, dude!"

Selby looked at Bodhi and said, "Just thank you; words can't say how I feel right now."

They all gathered around an uncomfortable Bodhi, slapping him on the back and making bad jokes. The festive attitude had returned, though each one of them knew they would never be the same and had a lot of processing to do.

Amy took Selby's face in both hands and said, "I love you so much—I was crazy scared."

"Amelia, you are the love of lifetimes, and I hope you know how important you are to me. Can we stay together for, at the very least, the rest of this lifetime?"

Amy smiled her beautiful smile for the first time in what seemed to be forever. She helped Selby get out of bed and led him down the hall to their room.

"C'mon, Sel, let's get you readjusted to the physical universe."

The End

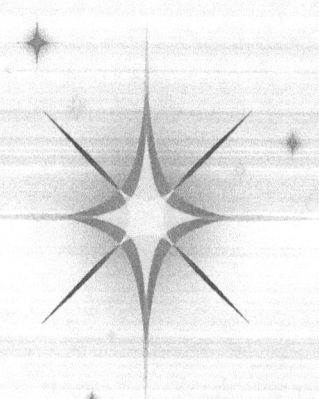

YOU CAN HELP

IT IS OVERDUE to create a future of peace and dignity for all. Please consider supporting The Prem Rawat Foundation's Food for People program, which prepares a nutritious hot meal daily for children living in poverty. They also provide eyeglasses to those without basic access to eye care. These programs have dramatically increased school attendance and also helped lift entire villages in India, Nepal and Africa out of poverty. TPRF sponsors the Peace Education Program in correctional facilities, homeless shelters, veteran's groups, and others in over seventy countries. The program gives participants an opportunity to focus and reflect on their understanding of inner peace and dignity.

Please consider supporting Sea Shepherd and Greenpeace for their efforts to save the biodiversity of the oceans and to re-wild the planet.

ACKNOWLEDGMENTS

FOREMOST, I would like to thank my wife, Gail, for her genuine overall encouragement. I would also like to thank my daughter, LaLita King, for her extraordinary cover art illustration.

A major shout out to Lisa Hebert, who helped with the story line and unknowingly convinced me to publish this story. Also, to Russ Kraus for helping with plot holes and for telling me while reading it, that he didn't want the story to end, and to Susan Kraus for her diligent help with the manuscript.

Thank you to the following who *unknowingly* helped the story development: Richard Donaldson, David Sweet, *The Expanse*, and *Star Trek*.

Cover Art: @kingfamilybooks

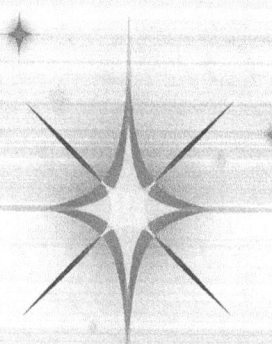

BOOK CLUB INVITATION

TO SHARE INSIGHTS with and answer questions from the readers of *The Saving of Verano,* Ken is available to speak via Zoom with your book club.

Please contact Ken through his website to schedule an appearance at your next book club meeting. Use the QR code below to be directed to his contact form.

Author website: KenHelfer.com

ABOUT THE AUTHOR

KEN HELFER is a self-educated writer. At nineteen, Helfer built a rustic cabin in the Ozark Mountains with hand tools while living off the grid. He spent his time reading anything and everything he could while living in the backwoods. After his time in the wilderness, he took on full-time volunteer work for several years all around the US and worked  with talented people from all over the world. Over the years, he started and ran three companies—all still in business. Helfer has enjoyed the trails and forests of this beautiful planet, mountain bike riding or hiking almost daily. He lives with his wife in Durango, Colorado.